CRAWLSPACE

Published by Clockwork Dragon Books
www.clockworkdragon.net

First printing, May 2019

Crawlspace is a work of fiction. People, places, and incidents are either products of the author's mind or used fictitiously. No endorsement of any kind should be inferred by existing locations or organizations within it.

No teenagers, spaceships, Marines, or aliens were harmed in the making of this book. We tore the crap out of the space station, though.

ISBN: 978-1-944334-37-6

HARPER REVOLUTION #2

CRAWLSPACE

LEE FRENCH

Clockwork Dragon Books

This series was inspired by the amazing, girl-positive music of Ilana Harkavy.

Thanks to the Clockwork Dragon crew and the Rebel Writers for all your support and awesomeness.

CHAPTER 1

Pulsing light from the wormhole faded. The mirror's surface revealed a coffee shop, static hazing the image in and out. I'd visited a place like it a thousand times. Black and brown dominated the decor with white and green accents. At the counter, a barista taking a woman's order glanced over her shoulder and squinted in my direction.

Maybe the barista saw a hazy version of the big gun-shaped thing pointed at the mirror. Between them, the air rippled as if superheated.

I could practically smell the cappuccino. The idea of a chocolate-dipped biscotti soaking in a latte danced on my tongue. And cheesecake. If I could have a slice of cheesecake, even without strawberry sauce, I could die happy.

The five of us—four Marines and me, the little sister—stood behind a protective glass wall, out of direct line of sight. Through that mirror's image, we could go home. Earth. We belonged there more than we belonged in some unknown region of space populated by at least seven other species. None of us knew the languages or customs, and all of us wanted to return to the familiarity of home.

Kind of. I had mixed feelings about it. The guys didn't, though. They'd all been out here for two years, so they'd had plenty of time to get frustrated and angry about this situation. I'd arrived maybe a week ago.

Baldwin smiled, lit up with joy for the first time since I'd met him. The redhead basked in the glow of escape, and probably could already taste clam chowder again. I'd heard everyone in New England liked that stuff. Even if he didn't, I had no doubt he'd take it over the weird slop we ate out here.

One step behind him, Nash pumped his deep bronze fist in the air. Victory glowed from every pore. He'd already helped me a ton, and I could take heart in knowing that making the wormhole device work had started to repay him.

After him, Mendez flashed me his cocky, charming Latinx grin with the wattage amped to eleven million. How could I hate going home when it made him so happy?

Ethan, my big brother, took my hand. I still couldn't decide if I dreamed about him or I'd really found him. I'd missed him so hard for so long. My best friend, my surrogate dad, my hero had gone MIA two years ago, and then alien tech had dropped me into his lap by mistake.

As we took our first steps toward the wormhole, Ethan tousled my red curls. His brilliant smile shone brighter than the other three guys put together.

Most MIA Marines never got to go home, but Sergeant Ethan Harper and his three remaining squadmates would.

We'd waited behind the glass in case my experimentation with the alien controls backfired. I couldn't read their symbols, and hadn't yet found a primer for how their tech worked. By using logic to the best of my ability, I'd gotten it right.

I had not "stumbled into" the correct configuration. Mostly, someone had already set up the system to bring people from Earth. My input had involved figuring out how to reverse its direction. In discovering how to do so, I'd learned the basics of how to program it.

The space station housing the wormhole generator rocked beneath our feet.

Baldwin dropped his alien tech laser rifle and rushed for the corner of the observation area. We'd waited behind it in case my experimentation caused unpredictable results. Nash and Mendez jumped into action behind him.

All light faded. Machine hum wound to nothing. The image of the coffee shop died. Everyone stumbled to a stop in darkness.

Part of me cheered. No more worrying about my crappy friends and crappy life! The rest of me knew how disappointing the guys would find this. We'd gone through so much to get to this point. One minute sooner and we all would've made it through.

Instead, we had to brace for impact without an escape plan. Figuring out how to restart the engines would help. Discovering why they'd shut off might also matter.

"Back to Akata," Ethan barked.

"She's gone," I said. Our sentient spaceship made from a colony of space coral with a hive mind had evacuated the area to keep herself safe. I knew this because she'd made me an armored suit of the coral to wear, and it had died when she'd put too much distance between us. In my pocket, I had a handful of bones from the dead pile of coral that had sloughed off my body.

The guys let out a collective breath, like they had to re-center or load a new program.

Ethan squeezed my hand. "We're going to assume hostiles shut down the engines."

Not my first guess. I thought something might've hit the station and knocked the solar panels offline. We'd find out soon, at least.

"We'll have to hole up before the power comes back so we can evaluate and plan. Baldwin, take point and lead us back to that room with the screens. Nash, rear. Mendez, you're watching over Emma." He let go of my hand and raised his rifle, readying it for use.

My four escorts snapped into soldier mode. Their black BDUs made them even harder to see under these conditions, but I could hear them. They muttered too low to understand over their radios and earbuds. Each man had a rifle to make click and *chk-chk*. Baldwin grunted.

All of us wore footwear resembling Marine combat boots. The guys had black ones. I had soft, shell pink boots to match my clothes. Despite the metal-like flooring, we made only light pattering sounds as we crept through the darkness.

Mendez took my hand and set it on his shoulder. I had to reach up, which meant I stayed close behind him. Like the other three guys, he stood about six feet tall, almost half a foot taller than me.

At this point, I knew how to follow a Marine—keep my mouth shut unless I had something important to say and don't do anything stupid.

Something touched my shoulder. I jumped, squeaked, and flushed with panic.

"It's me," Nash whispered with his Southern drawl. From the rear. Where Ethan told him to go. Behind me.

Way to panic over nothing, Emma. I took a deep breath and nodded. Which he couldn't see, of course. "Sorry," I murmured.

"You're good. Keep moving."

We slipped to the door with Baldwin in the lead. As soon as he hauled open the big, creaking door, dim red light spilled onto us. I took my hand off Mendez's shoulder. Nash squeezed mine and let go. Both guys shifted enough to give me a bubble of personal space.

Baldwin checked through the door and led us into the corridor. As we hurried along the left wall, I heard the station's metal groaning and creaking. Something clanked in the distance, the sound bouncing around enough that I couldn't determine anything about it.

We stopped at a corner and waited while Baldwin peered around it. He gave a signal, then we followed him past it. This repeated several times before we reached the bottom of a set of stairs meeting a perpendicular corridor.

Once again, Baldwin peered in both directions. He

held up a hand, then jerked his thumb backward. I heard nothing besides the groan of large things shifting against each other. Then I caught the murmur of distant voices.

Mendez tugged on my arm. We backed into the previous corridor.

When everyone had reached the top of the stairs again, Ethan frowned at the wall. "Ideas?" he whispered.

We didn't have a map of the station. Finding the wormhole room had taken luck. It hadn't even been our goal. I'd hoped to discover enough information to piece together how to use the wormhole device. Instead, we'd walked into the room and I'd fiddled with the controls until I thought I'd reversed it. If we ever had another chance to use that device, I could make it take us home to Earth.

I didn't know anything else about it yet, including how to find a new path to reach it from anywhere else on the station. Or, more importantly at the moment, to reach anywhere else from it.

The voices down the stairs grew louder.

"Just pick a direction," I whispered.

Ethan gave me a curt nod and pointed at the last intersection. Baldwin plunged down the corridor. We followed. After pausing at another few corners, he took a set of stairs up and kept going.

At an intersection, we found one of the station's many robots. The six-foot tall machine used two tank-like treads to move. Four long, folding arms, each mounted on one side of a cube, ended with two pairs of pincers. Below the cube, a dark, glassy sphere anchored to the treads by a stubby column.

This one stood inert, where I'd deactivated it from a control room I'd vandalized. We called that place the "screens room" because it had a ton of screens. Mendez whacked the robot with the butt of his rifle as we hurried past. The clunk echoed off the walls, ceiling, and floor in every direction. It had no other effect.

Ethan paused to glare at Mendez. He flashed a cheesy

grin. I smacked his arm. Baldwin kept moving.

These corridors had the fewest doors I'd seen in a hallway on this station so far. In other sections, they always had a reasonable interval, like thirty or forty feet, and on both sides. This area had a door every hundred feet or so, on one side only.

What would anyone put in a space station without frequent access points? My efforts to learn enough engineering and astrophysics to build space-worthy ships gave me a basis to guess, but aliens had constructed this facility. Humans designed things to accommodate humans.

So far, I knew these aliens wanted to ensure the survival of a wide variety of creatures with differing physiological needs. They didn't want to make any of us comfortable, though. These aliens brought creatures through their wormhole device to enslave them. For what purpose, we didn't know, except that Ethan and the guys thought they'd been pointed at other aliens for battle.

Since I'd seen the detention area, I knew we hadn't wandered into that. That section had lots of doors with cells big enough to hold a dozen or so humans. Like the twelve men who'd come through two years ago. Ethan, Nash, Baldwin, and Mendez were all that remained of a Marines squad deployed in Afghanistan.

No one had found their bodies, so the report had indicated Ethan as MIA, presumed dead. Since their abduction, eight of those men had fulfilled that presumption.

Engines. The engines might not need frequent access, especially if they used a process fleshy beings couldn't withstand long. I knew the station used solar power from the nearby star. I hadn't seen turbines or engines yet, so I didn't know what processes they used to translate that into functioning machines.

We passed another inert robot.

Maybe thirty feet past the second robot, Baldwin stopped at a recessed door and tried to open it. His effort didn't work, so he moved on.

As I reached the door, I checked it. The cell door I'd seen had used a lock and hinges similar to human ones. This door looked more advanced because it didn't have visible hinges or any kind of handle. That meant it needed power to function.

The door to the engine room needed power to function. I covered my mouth to smother a giggle.

No, okay, these aliens had more engineering knowledge than me, so they'd done this for a reason. Anyone who could build a device capable of punching through space-time deserved the benefit of the doubt, even if their robots used treadmill bases.

I stopped to examine the door frame.

Nash nudged my shoulder.

Holding up a finger to ask him to wait, I ran my other hand over the section at the right height for a handle. A panel swiveled under the slight pressure, revealing a lever. I pulled it. The door clicked ajar.

This door not only didn't need power, it actually had hinges on the inside and a latch, like any regular door. The construction had concealed this fact from me. Stupid aliens.

As he pointed for me to step aside, Nash hissed to the rest of the group.

Baldwin jogged to the door and held his rifle ready. Ethan reached it on his heels. Mendez hauled me further from the spot. With two men flanking it and brandishing their weapons, I realized they meant to do some kind of commando door breach.

Ethan kicked the door wide open. Baldwin ducked and spun inside. Ethan followed him. Nash stepped inside after Ethan. The door swung closed behind them without latching again.

Mendez and I stayed outside, leaning against the wall beside the door and watching down the corridor in both directions. My heart thundered in my chest, expecting aliens to find us any moment. They'd traipse around the corner, see us, shoot, and take Mendez and me prisoner.

Worse visions danced in my head, of what the guys found inside the room. Way to go, Emma! If anyone could figure out how to open a door to a deathtrap, it would have to be me. The aliens had similar physiology to us, but that didn't mean they had all the same tolerances. A small room could have a wildly different temperature or mix of elements in the air.

My stomach clenched at the thought of all three men lying on the floor, gasping for breath in an environment with too much nitrogen or ammonia, or whatever else the aliens might prefer.

Through the open door, I heard Baldwin say, "Clear." He dropped the end of the word like anyone from certain parts of New England.

Noticing I'd held my breath, I gasped for air.

"Clear," Ethan echoed.

"Clear," Nash rumbled.

I let Mendez go first in case he felt a need to be manly. As I reached the door again, I noticed a tiny green light flashing on the nearby robot. Quiet whirs and clicks echoed from it.

Whoever had arrived and knocked the station offline had activated the robots.

Dealing with one of those robots took more oomph than I could muster. I hurried through the door. Ethan shut it.

"The robots are coming online," I whispered.

CHAPTER 2

Trembling in the walls and a low hum announced the engines restarting. Any second, the cameras would restart, providing the aliens with video and audio of every corridor in the station.

We'd found a place to hide just in time. I leaned against the door of a small room with lockers lining the walls. Nash stood in front of another closed door to the side. Baldwin opened a locker and peered at the contents.

White light flickered on overhead. As usual for this place, we couldn't see any fixtures—the light came from everywhere and nowhere. Everyone grumbled and shielded their eyes, including me.

Engine noise grew until we'd have to almost shout to hear each other. This confirmed my guess about the section of the ship we'd wandered into. At least, I thought it did. Knowing that, I had a decent guess for our relative location on the cylindrical station. Not that this information helped me much. I still didn't know how to get anyplace in particular.

I pointed at the second door and raised my brow at Nash.

He pushed it. The door slid into the wall. Noise blasted us. A gray, metal-like catwalk ran alongside a long tube with a zillion indicator lights, screens, and porthole handles studding the length of it.

When I flashed him a thumbs-up, he shut the door again. Someone had put a lot of effort into making that door buffer noise.

Baldwin held up an object reminiscent of a screwdriver. "Tools."

My favorite magic word made me grin. I rushed to the locker, shoved his big, muscle-bound self aside, and stuck my face into the compartment.

Every tool hung on a hook or lay on a shelf with an outline showing what belonged there.

"It's Christmas," I squealed. Most than half of the treasures had no obvious purpose I knew of, but I recognized the simple tools. Aliens used hammers too, apparently.

"I'm glad somebody's happy," Nash grunted.

Mendez checked the rest of the lockers, one by one, and left the doors open. "She figured it out once. She can make it work again."

"One minute," Baldwin grumbled.

Right. These guys had seen their dream of going home snatched from them in the cruelest way possible. After two years out here, after watching their friends die, after giving up hope, I'd fallen into their laps by accident. I'd handed them a victory by figuring out how to work the machine. They'd tasted it.

Ethan leaned against the outer door with his rifle across his chest, brooding at the floor.

Nash stood vigilant at the inner door.

Baldwin glared at me. "You don't want to go home."

I froze in the middle of inspecting a triangular Allen-style wrench. The intensity of his anger made me want to crawl into a hole forever. Never mind the fact that no, I didn't want to go home. Did he really think I'd keep them from leaving so I could stay? Had I given the impression of that much selfishness?

"Settle down," Ethan snapped. "She didn't shut off the power."

"She stalled." Baldwin stabbed a finger at me.

"I did not!" I thought about throwing the wrench at him, but it was small and wouldn't accomplish anything. Instead, I stuffed it into my pocket. "I did the best I could. It's not like I can read their language. And I'm not a software person! I'm an engineer. I build things and take things apart, and I figure out how to make things work. I did it as fast as I could."

"How do we know?"

Mendez pushed down Baldwin's arm. "It's not her fault."

"I know why he's jumping to her defense." Baldwin pointed at Ethan, who rolled his eyes. "But why are you doing it?"

"Because she doesn't deserve this." Mendez shoved Baldwin's shoulder. "You want to blame someone, blame the blue-skins. All of this is their fault. If not for them, we could be home now."

I'd met one of the aliens responsible for this space station. He'd had blue skin and two antennae instead of ears. Otherwise, he'd resembled a human by a surprising amount.

Baldwin grunted and shoved Mendez in return. Mendez raised a fist.

"Knock it off," Ethan growled with his finger on the button for his radio.

Both men stopped in mid-motion, glaring at each other. Mendez lowered his fist. Baldwin sat on the floor in a huff.

"I hate these guys," Nash said.

Ethan sighed. "We all do. If not for them, we'd have gone home and deployed again by now."

"I miss—" Mendez glanced at me, then shook his head. "I miss the sand. Blowing in your face. Grit getting into everything, even your socks and shorts. Waiting for your turn to complain about it because—"

All four men intoned together, "—if everyone

complains at the same time, I'm gonna beat the crap outta alla you jarheads."

Their squad leader must've said that enough times to turn it into a joke. As far as I knew, they'd watched that guy die out here.

"I'm sorry we didn't get home today," I said, trying to show Baldwin that I meant it. Because I did, except for the "we" part. I wanted him to get home. They all deserved to go home and see their families again. "But Mendez is right. Now that I know how to do it, I can make it work much faster next time. No guessing or experimenting."

"We just have to wait for the aliens to leave." Ethan patted a pants pocket. "That's why we brought our MREs."

I didn't think we had enough water to last long on the station. After a day or two, I suspected everyone would suffer from impaired judgment, and then we'd do something stupid. We'd get caught. Whatever I could think of to try, we needed to try it now, not as a last resort.

The guys, though, needed time to regroup. I recognized this kind of defeat because I felt it every time I ate the last bite of cheesecake slathered in strawberry sauce.

My mouth watered at the thought of it. I swallowed and turned my back on them, thankful I couldn't indulge. If I didn't eat the cheesecake, I didn't have to purge it.

Wait. No. I knew I had a problem, so I'd covered step one. Now I needed to move to step two, which I figured should involve not letting myself imagine purging. Or if I did, only think about the bad parts.

The bad parts of purging included…um…still thinking…

"Cog, are you going to do something with that, or just stare at it really hard?"

Ethan's question jarred me from my train of thought. That worked for getting my mind off the subject, so I ran with it.

I'd picked up a flat, hinged box in a semicircle shape

and turned it over in my hands. "I don't know what it is." I tried pressing on every part of the thing and nothing happened. It reminded me of an artifact from a horror movie that started the apocalypse or unleashed the devil, or something equally unpleasant.

Ethan shrugged. "Then put it back and keep looking. We've got time."

How could I put down something classified as a tool when I didn't know its functions? Marines. If you can't figure out how to kill someone with it, forget about it, I guess.

I dropped the thing on the floor. It clattered and popped open. On the floor lay a flat thing shaped like a putty knife. The box configuration had obscured both the handle and the blade. For a few seconds, I stared at the unexpected find on a space station with metal walls and floors.

Picking it up by the handle, I tried to think of anything I'd seen that might use this tool. Nothing came to mind. They had no drywall. The locker had no spackle or tubs of similar material. I fussed with it and poked it until I cut my finger on the edge.

The sharp, short pain made me squeak. Ethan appeared by my side with lightning reflexes and inspected my bleeding finger.

"It's nothing," I huffed. When I tugged on my hand, he let go. I sucked on the tiny cut.

Ethan shrugged. "Sure. Until you get tetanus. I'll check you for a fever later."

I stuck out my tongue at him. He rolled his eyes and gave me more space.

Taking care to avoid the sharp edge, I figured out how to refold the putty knife and stuck it into my pocket with the triangle tool. Even if it wanted to open, the fabric, tight over my gross, fat thigh, would keep it shut.

With my finger still in my mouth, I returned to rifling through the locker. My next selection resembled a power screwdriver small enough to need a cord, yet lacking one. I pointed it at the wall because I'm not stupid and pushed the button on the end. The noise it made sounded exactly like a tiny power drill, except I didn't see a bit. Twisting the shank made the bit pop out.

No one in their right mind would make a single-size drill. As I twisted it more, the bit shrank. The size ran from the width of my pinky to that of a hole in a button. The mechanism seemed clunky to me, but a lot of the station seemed that way to me. With the bit recessed again, I handed it to Mendez.

If we returned to Akata, I wanted pants with lots of pockets. My current pants, pink leggings made of a soft, loose material, had two front pockets and no others. I wanted at least six roomy pockets, plus loops or thin pockets for tools like this drill.

Going through several other objects, I discovered a small device with a readout that I suspected measured volts and ohms. Aside from a thick length of metal or gray space coral—or an alloy of the two—similar to a crowbar, nothing else seemed useful or interesting for the moment. We had time, though, so I picked up each thing and cataloged in my head what I thought it did.

Once I'd rifled through every locker, I straightened and said the most dangerous words ever.

"I have an idea."

CHAPTER 3

Baldwin sneered at me. "Great. We can go snatch defeat from the jaws of victory again."

"Look, I'm sorry the aliens busted up our party like parents coming home early from vacation," I snapped. "That really isn't my fault. We weren't even going to try using the machine on this trip, remember? We were going to scout so I could get enough information to figure out how to do it on another run. That's still my goal here."

"We're stranded, princess," Baldwin grumbled. "There won't be another run."

"Akata will come back for us." I planted my fists on my hips. "She told me she would, and I believe her. We just need a way to let her know we're still here and need a pickup."

Ethan raised his brow. Mendez let a hint of a smile show. Nash gave me a once-over, then nodded with his face still set in a serious cast. Baldwin crossed his arms and stayed grumpy.

So long as I explained well enough, Ethan would back me, Mendez wouldn't argue, and Nash would go along with whatever Ethan said. Baldwin would probably disagree no matter what right now. If I thought waiting would make him more agreeable, I would've waited.

"The engines are operational, which means everything is operational, right? The station has ways to send signals, and it also has lights. If we can find the controls for one of those things, I can use it to send a signal to Akata. She probably won't be able to respond, even if she's close, and we'll have to wait until she considers it safe enough to approach. But we'll be able to board her again."

Nash turned and listened. I counted that as a victory. Mendez's smile grew thoughtful. Baldwin continued to grump in the corner.

"Once we can do that, Akata can help us sort out the most efficient path to the wormhole device room. I should be able to get enough information for her to help me deal with the robots and cameras for that insertion too. Which will make it much faster and easier when we come back for the real wormhole attempt. We'll be able to get in and home before they even realize we're here and doing anything."

Ethan nodded. "Sounds good to me. I don't think we can use the control room we found before, so what are you intending to look for?"

"The actual devices, or where they connect to the system."

"You want to follow the wires," Mendez said.

"More or less." The plan called for me probably doing a fair number of risky things. I mentioned none of this. The less Ethan knew about the details, the better.

Mendez patted Ethan's arm. "Like the time when we found where those so-called security cameras fed to."

"Except without the explosives," Nash said.

"Yes," I nodded. "Let's not use explosives. Since we'll probably have to work near the hull."

All four men—yes, even Baldwin—chuckled like I'd stumbled into an inside joke.

Marines.

"Since they definitely have cameras on the corridors, we should try going through the engine room." I pointed at the door beside Nash.

"Let's find out," Ethan said. "Baldwin, on your feet and

let's do this."

Still hunched and growly, Baldwin asked, "What if we get caught?"

Ethan shrugged. "Then we get caught. You going to give up because it's long odds, Marine? Or are you going to suck it up and deal with the best chance we've got? Because you can stay here if you want. The rest of us are going."

God, these guys had issues.

Sure, Emma, because you're perfect.

My stomach growled as if it heard me. We didn't have time to eat right now. Food could wait. I didn't really need it anyway. I'd eaten so much before this foray that I could last another three days if I needed to.

Baldwin stood with a grunt and gripped his rifle.

Nash pushed a block of green crap into my hand. "Stop thinking. Eat. Bolt it because it tastes weird."

"What is it?"

Opening the door, Nash shrugged with a smartass grin. Noise overwhelmed us so no one could answer.

Jerk. I stared at the weird bar.

Ethan took my hand and moved it toward my mouth, bar and all. He raised his brow as if to tell me he'd force-feed me if I didn't eat it of my own free will.

I supposed if Baldwin could get off his ass despite his cranky objections, I could stuff some food of dubious nature into my face.

The first bite of chewy green stuff reminded me of the disaster of a pumpkin pie Aunt Carrie had made a few years ago for Thanksgiving. She'd forgotten all the spices and somehow had made it so thick we could only cut it with a knife. Gross didn't cover it. Weird did. Nobody had batted an eye at me spitting out the pie because they all did it too.

This bar, though, I forced myself to swallow. Knowing these guys, it had vitamins, minerals, protein, and fat. That last thing made me want to gag.

Mendez draped an arm over my shoulders and made

me start walking across a catwalk beside a giant tube. Through the holes, I could see black strips of wiring under our feet. Overhead, another catwalk pointed to an upper level. Something rippled through the holes in that higher grid like a clear barrier of water.

Leaning close, Mendez said, "We don't have anything else, chica, so you better down the whole thing."

What he didn't say spoke volumes more than what he did.

They all knew I had…a problem. The problem starts with the letter "b" and ends with the letter "ulimia." Bulimia. For almost two years, I'd used porcelain bowls to purge the calories I didn't deserve or need. Anything with strawberry sauce, anything thick with fat, anything that made life worth living…

Looking back at myself on Earth, sitting with my friends and feeling fat and worthless, I think maybe I might've killed myself soon if I hadn't fallen through a wormhole in my bathroom mirror to land at Ethan's feet on an alien space station far, far away from home.

Nash had figured out all this from watching me for less than a week, and I'd admitted it out loud for the first time about two hours ago. Since they knew and I knew they knew, I figured I could expect a lot of oversight from them about food.

For example, Mendez reminding me to eat with a vague threat attached.

While we walked alongside the large tube, the noise too overpowering to hear anything else, I covered my mouth so I wouldn't spit out the green bar. Each bite took a force of will and felt like torture. I enjoyed eating food that tasted good. Sure, I usually ruined it by sending it back up, but if I had to suffer, at least I did it for something worthwhile.

This crap, I had to choke down and keep down.

Mendez didn't let go of me until I swallowed the last bite. Then he kissed the top of my head and moved forward so

I followed him.

Before he enlisted, Ethan had kissed the top of my head every night before bed. He'd done it to protect me from nightmares, or so he'd said. When it didn't work, I used to sneak into his room and crawl into his bed. His body had always blazed with heat. Without waking up, he'd manage to drape an arm over me while I clung to his warmth.

If Mom or Dad had ever found us like that, they probably would've thought all kinds of wrong things.

I tried to imagine Mom coming to wake me, finding my bed empty, and freaking out. She'd never once done anything like it, though. Dad never did either. Our parents didn't go up to the third floor of our house, where Ethan and I had our bedrooms, a shared space for the TV and school work, and a shared bathroom.

After my tenth birthday, the closest either of them ever came to invading our space was shouting from the second floor landing. Before then, Mom would come up to tuck me in at bedtime. Then I hit double digits. Suddenly, I was a big girl.

No, Mom, ten-year-old me hadn't been a big girl. Where Mom and Dad failed, Ethan had stepped in. He'd helped me with my homework. I'd helped him build models of spacecraft, including the Soyuz capsule and Apollo module. When Mom and Dad worked late, he'd led our efforts to make dinner, showing me how to make pasta, grilled cheese sandwiches, and fifteen other things I didn't dare eat anymore.

Even though I didn't miss home, I really missed cheese. Cheesecake. Strawberry sauce. Lemon pound cake. Fluffy, crunchy biscuits drenched with melted butter.

Ugh. I needed to stop thinking about food and anything other than finding the right wires to send signals to Akata.

I needed to think about my parents as much as they thought about me—not at all.

CHAPTER 4

Baldwin found a twenty-foot ladder to the level above. He and Ethan shouldered their rifles and climbed it without a second thought. Despite the opalescent barrier covering the hole. Did the guys not see it, or had they experienced enough not to find anything strange about a writhing membrane of clear water?

When Baldwin reached the barrier, he stuck an arm through to his elbow, then withdrew it. His limb appeared intact and unharmed. Like any other Marine would do, he shrugged and climbed through the barrier.

On the other side, his shape turned hazy and indistinct, as if he'd plunged into murky water. Upward. I waited for him to sputter into view, or reach with a hand for rescue. He didn't.

I glanced at Nash behind me and did my best to convey my concern about the barrier with body language. Nash shrugged and shooed me onward. Because nothing says "safe" like a weird thing doing weird things.

Mendez and Nash had a short conversation without using words. I couldn't make out any of it, except it had something to do with the ladder. At the end, Nash shrugged and hit the ladder first. Mendez would follow me.

Apparently, he felt his job of keeping an eye on me made this arrangement important. Ethan had noticed the discussion and hadn't tried to intervene, so he maybe agreed or didn't think it mattered.

As soon as Nash climbed high enough, I gulped and put my hands on the ladder.

"You good?" Mendez shouted at me.

Above, Ethan plunged through the barrier.

If something happened to him, I thought I wanted it to also happen to me. Besides, the two blobby shapes overhead moved and remained coherent. They didn't thrash like someone in pain would or fall to the floor.

Nodding to Mendez, I focused on climbing. Foot, arm, foot, arm, repeat and breathe. Halfway, one of my boots slipped. I clung to the ladder. How did that even happen with the thick treads? Emma's physical incompetence strikes again!

Mendez climbed around me. For a moment, I thought he meant to leave me behind like the loser I am. My friends would've done that. I could imagine more than one of them stepping on my face as they kept going.

Then he stopped with his arms around my waist. He pressed close, cocooning my lower body with strength and warmth. "I got you!"

These guys weren't my friends back home. They acted a lot different. Decent. Human. Kind.

With Mendez supporting me, I climbed the rest of the way. I screwed my eyes shut as I raised a hand through the barrier. The sensation reminded me of pushing a gauze curtain. Since it didn't hurt and the other side felt like regular air, I grabbed the next rung and lifted my head through.

I opened my eyes. Ethan crouched beside the hole and smiled at me. The noise remained deafening.

Ethan took my hand and helped me until I put my feet on the new floor. Mendez swarmed through the barrier and to his feet in half a second. He, Ethan, and Nash exchanged non-words. The "conversation" ended with all three flashing a thumbs-up.

With Nash behind me again, we followed the new tube

back in the direction we'd come, except twenty feet higher. This level, I noted, had doors opposite the tube, spaced at regular intervals of about forty feet. Smaller pipes, the kind that might shield wires or carry some low-flow liquid or gas, ran along the wall, over the doors.

For several steps, I debated trying to cut into one of those smaller tubes. We had the crowbar-like thing, and it had enough of a sharp edge on one end to try. The material presenting as metal actually had some properties of plastic, making it easier to chop through. They made it from gray space coral, and probably other things mixed in.

Screw it. I wanted to know.

Holding up a hand to get Nash to pause, I stopped and moved closer to the wall. I poked the pipe. To my surprise, it yielded like a thick membrane full of water. Cutting it would probably cause a problem. The bad kind.

Never mind on the pipe. Maybe I could find an access port and discover its contents without potentially flooding the engine room or covering myself in toxic slime.

Nash shrugged as I mouthed an apology. The rest of the guys hadn't noticed my brief detour. We caught up, I panted from jogging for ten seconds, and everyone kept walking.

Baldwin and Ethan stopped at a dead-end door like the one below. They used a lot of hand gestures, and it looked like an argument about which way to go.

I doubted Baldwin cared about my opinion, so I didn't wade in to provide it. Instead, I took a closer look at the screens along the engine tube. Messing with them didn't seem smart, so I'd ignored them so far. With nothing better to do other than watch two grown men using Marine sign language to yell at each other, though, I didn't see any harm in examining one.

The screens used the same set of symbols I'd seen on everything else in this facility. I'd figured out a few things through trial and error. With Akata's help, I thought I could piece together a fair amount of the language.

Whenever we returned to Akata, of course.

My selected screen showed five horizontal lines equally spaced from top to bottom. Near the left edge, three of the five lines showed a down spike and the other two showed an up spike. The lines otherwise stayed steady.

This graph had recorded the engine shutdown by five metrics I couldn't identify. Which meant it monitored the engines. Monitoring activity wouldn't cause an engine shutdown, so I poked one line with a fingertip.

Damn, my nails needed work. Since arriving in this galaxy, I'd broken every single one. All had ragged, snarly edges. The pink polish I used to keep myself from chewing on them had chipped enough to look stupid.

Beneath my disgusting, jagged fingernails, the single line expanded to fill the entire screen. The down spike had more nuance, showing a sharp, immediate plunge followed by a jagged, four stage climb back to normal.

I tapped the bottom of the dip. In that spot, a small filled rectangle appeared with a dotted line leading to three lines of text. If I could read any of it, I had no doubt the text would prove informative. Probably, it indicated the engines had gone offline, maybe with a note about how or why.

For several seconds, I stared at those alien characters, trying to memorize them. Then I tapped on another point for more data. I tapped each point. They gave me more samples of alien writing.

When I finally looked up, pleased with myself, I discovered everyone staring at me with varying degrees of impatience. Baldwin, predictably, showed the most in his narrow-eyed glare and tapping foot.

Ethan gestured like a host toward the door as if to ask if we could move on yet.

Too much noise to talk had its upsides.

Tapping in the upper right corner returned the screen to how I'd found it. Because I could, I held up a finger and did all the same things with a second line, this one with an upward spike. Then I did it with a third line.

I may have done the third one to annoy the guys more than to gather data.

Once I finished, I returned the screen to start and stepped away from it. Mendez smirked as he shooed me against the wall. This section didn't have a door. I took advantage of my position to prod the pipe again, then several different spots below it. The pipe remained weirdly fluid. Every spot I checked on the wall seemed solid.

Ethan, Baldwin, and Nash breached the door.

Setting my palm on the wall and sliding it back and forth revealed nothing. Unlike other parts of the facility, which had walls made of panels, this one appeared to be made of solid material.

Mendez tapped me on the shoulder. He led me through the door. We stepped into a tiny room, big enough to hold both of us and nothing else. The door shut behind us. Harsh, cold air blasted from every direction. Before it stopped, Mendez grabbed me and held me close, protecting my face.

The front wall slid open. We stumbled through. Mendez kept me from slipping and falling. The engine noise cut off. My ears rang with the sudden silence.

"You might've warned us," Mendez groused.

"Get your hands off her," Ethan said.

Mendez let go. "She almost fell over."

"Sure she did." Ethan wrapped a big hand around my arm and swung me to face him.

I yanked against his grip. "You told him to watch over me. He watched over me."

Ethan released me and huffed.

Without Mendez's body providing heat, I shivered. That frigid blast hadn't done me any good. I saw Mendez roll his eyes at Ethan's back, so I figured Ethan must've glared at him.

Boys.

We stood in a room with a dozen blue gas masks and white hazmat suits hanging on hooks. The aliens considered something in the engine room hazardous enough to require protective measures. Since I hadn't noticed anything, I supposed it might emit radiation.

Whatever they felt a need to protect themselves from, the membrane under the catwalk kept it contained on one level or the other. We probably hadn't stayed in the room long enough for it to matter. Add the decontamination procedure and I didn't see a reason to worry. After all, the membrane didn't prevent people from passing through.

I lifted a hazmat glove attached to the nearest suit. The material felt like a cross between rubber and steel. "Now that we know this room is safe, I should go back through to check more stuff." Did I need a suit? Probably not. I'd wear one anyway. The glove had ridged fingertips, which suggested it could operate the touchscreens.

"No." Ethan pointed to the outer door. "We need to find a secure location. This area might have cameras, and they could walk in here at any moment."

"We should make a run on the wormhole device," Baldwin said. "They'd never expect that."

Somehow, I doubted the aliens would leave that room unguarded. Baldwin, though, wouldn't listen to me. I shrugged.

Ethan frowned at the floor. "We're going to work on keeping moving until we're sure we have a secure place to hide. If that brings us close enough to try the wormhole room, then we'll try it. Otherwise, the goal is to either find what Emma needs or to hide until the aliens leave."

Sergeant Harper knew how to strike a compromise to keep his troops happy, at least. I couldn't find fault with this new objective.

CHAPTER 5

I dropped the glove and watched it bobble back into place. "What if we wear these suits? As a disguise, I mean."

Nash prodded one with his rifle. "I don't see how we'd stick out less. These are probably for emergencies in the engine room. They wouldn't use them anywhere else."

"We don't know that," Mendez said. "Even if it just confuses them for a minute or two, isn't that worth it?"

"You always side with her," Baldwin grumbled.

"She's the smartest person in this room. Why shouldn't I?"

Nobody complimented me like that. They called me pretty or they said envious things about my red curls. People didn't comment on my brain power without also commenting on my appearance. Even Ethan had connected the two, comparing me to Hedy Lamarr in a way that made me feel like I had to live up to her legacy somehow. If I didn't build some groundbreaking space engine and also star in movies, I'd failed in his estimation.

Ethan smacked Mendez on the arm. "Knock it off."

"Knock what off? How am I the one who needs to stop?" Mendez pointed at Baldwin. "He's the crank here. I'm saying nice things about your sister."

"That's right, she's my sister." Ethan glared at Mendez, half-daring him to start a fight.

Yep, these guys had issues. That yoinked chance at going home had messed with them. If we had Akata, she'd help them sort through this stuff. We needed her more than ever, or we needed to go home.

"Guys, relax." I held up both hands, hoping they wouldn't see me as attacking them. "You're all jumpy. I don't need a boyfriend or a guardian for my virtue, I just need some slack."

The guys stared at me like they'd forgotten I could speak. Thanks, guys. Way to turn a compliment into a question about my competence.

"I just think they'll definitely know it's us without the suits," I said. "With the suits, they'll have to investigate whether they've had a containment breach or something first. By the time they confirm there isn't a malfunction, we can maybe find a hideout."

Mendez gestured as if to proclaim me Exhibit A in his case. "That's sound logic."

Nash shrugged. "I agree. That makes sense. We won't be able to run, but we'll be able to roam freely, at least for a while."

"Fine," Baldwin grumbled. He yanked a suit off the wall and set aside his rifle.

I took more care while collecting a suit for myself. Ethan helped me into mine, and I helped him into his.

My suit hung off my shoulders, baggy and loose like a scarecrow walked inside it. The face mask smelled like dirty socks, and the air I breathed through it tasted metallic. My thighs touched when I moved, making a corduroy *vwip* noise. Gross.

The guys strapped their rifles to their muscular thighs to conceal them inside the suits. When we finished, we all looked like we belonged in a movie about a plague outbreak.

Baldwin took point again as we stepped through the door, acting like we belonged. Nothing to see here, alien people. No fugitive human slaves wandering in the facility.

Only blue-skin aliens doing things they needed to do to keep the facility in good working order.

We strode up the corridor. A robot trundled past, ignoring us. My plan had at least worked in the short term.

This part of the facility didn't seem familiar to me. I'd examined what the guys knew of the layout with Akata's help, and though much of it looked the same, this part didn't have anything marking it as a place they'd visited before.

Baldwin turned a corner to the left, then turned one to the right. I wondered if he hoped we'd get captured. At least then he'd know his role.

Ethan patted his arm and pointed to a door. Baldwin shrugged. Mendez guided me to the wall to stay out of the way. As I stood there, watching my big brother and his men breach a door without weapons in hand, I realized Mendez wanted me to stay out of the line of fire. If anything shot through the open door, he intended for me to avoid getting hit and have the option to run.

The guys slipped inside. Nash followed a beat behind. Mendez waited with me.

Maybe this approach worked against humans with human weapons and gadgets, but I wondered how effective it would prove against an alien species with the technology to generate wormholes and block radiation or toxins with thin membranes. Especially since the guys didn't pause and wonder if maybe they shouldn't tempt fate by, say, plunging through a rippling layer of unknown stuff.

So far, nothing bad had happened to them.

Nash ran back out of the room, ripping off his hazmat suit. "Robot!"

See? I knew that tactic wouldn't work how they expected.

"Help me get my rifle," Mendez snapped.

I yanked open the back of his suit. Even a pathetic weakling like me could handle that.

Mendez ripped out his rifle and plunged into the

room. Which also seemed dumb to me. At least he kept the gas mask on his face. Nash followed on his heels, his rifle also freed.

Worried the robot might trundle out of the room, I turned around and walked away from the ill-chosen room. At the next corner, I stopped and peered around it. Two blue-skin aliens approached. Had they seen me? Probably.

As fast as my legs could carry me, I ran back to the room with the robot. Then I kept going past it and slipped around another corner. After checking the narrow corridor I'd ducked into and finding it empty, I pulled off my gas mask and used as small a slice of myself as possible to watch for the two aliens.

They had rounded the corner right after me. The pair carried small objects similar in size and shape to an electric razor, which I knew as stun weapons, and they hurried to the robot room.

Impulse one wanted me to flee and save myself.

Impulse two demanded I keep those two aliens from going into that room and stunning all four guys.

Ethan would've ordered me to obey impulse one. Perversely, knowing that made me want to follow impulse two.

Not sure what I could do without getting myself caught too fast, I opened my mouth and screamed as the two aliens reached the door. My shrill, high-pitched shriek caused them both to freeze.

The only thing in my hands was the gas mask. I threw it into the intersection and ran away. When I reached the next corner, I stopped again and peered back the way I'd come.

One alien scanned the narrow corridor. The other prodded the gas mask with his shoe. Like the first blue-skin alien I'd seen, these had bright blue flesh, dark, spiky hair, and two antennae sticking out of their foreheads instead of ears. They wore matching black, form-fitted jumpsuits with dark blue trim.

If they wore a uniform, did that mean military?

The two aliens spoke. I didn't understand any of it. They turned away from the corridor, though, and appeared intent on chasing down the guys instead of me.

I made a loud whimpery noise, like a pathetic groan, and ran again. As I bolted for the next corner, I struggled to free myself from the hazmat suit.

Great idea, Emma. Brilliant. Yes, let's evade the robots for five minutes so we can all struggle with the stupid suits at the worst possible moment. Genius.

The sleeve ripped, making a noise loud enough to wake the dead. I dove around the next corner and struggled to get my arm out of the torn sleeve. But I took the side that would lead them away from the guys. Leading them back in that direction defeated my purpose.

As I turned the next corner, yanking my arm out of the other sleeve, I ran into something. Someone. A different alien and I collided at high speed. My body bounced off them, then bounced off the wall. I stumbled into a different wall and fell backward.

Apparently, I had a penchant for finding nooks and crannies in this place, because this had happened to me before.

Last time, I'd fallen into an elevator intended to deliver a robot to its charging dock. This time, I tumbled head-first down a chute. Holding in a scream, I tried to wriggle around so I'd land feet-first. The chute didn't have enough space.

I panicked. Thumping my hands, elbows, feet, and knees against the tunnel walls, I screamed. If it didn't let me out, I'd die. Did the walls narrow to close me in tighter?

Yes. Yes, they did.

CHAPTER 6

The chute dumped me into a pile of something not quite soft and not quite hard. Like a heap of dirty laundry or a wadded flannel blanket. Dim red light glowed from everywhere and nowhere. I smelled rotting meat. My panting breaths came out as puffs in the frigid air.

Why the heck had someone put a laundry chute in that hallway? And why did it smell this bad?

Flailing my arms and legs, I discovered I'd landed in a room big enough for me not to hit the walls or ceiling. This calmed my panic. I breathed. The stench hit me with the force of a brick to the gut.

I would not throw up. I would not throw up. I would not throw up.

The fact I wanted to refuse to barf surprised me. Who could've predicted that? Not me.

Sitting up, I shook my head at myself. Purging? Good. Vomiting because of a stench? Bad.

No, I know. Purging is also bad. Work in progress.

I rubbed my face with my remaining hazmat sleeve. What made that stench? Something gross, no doubt. Did I want to see what I'd landed on? Maybe?

Cringing, I glanced down. Underneath me, the floor had regular, angled grooves angled to a point, like a closed camera iris. Something with that type of construction seemed designed to open. Probably, the stench came from the room below. I didn't want to find out for sure.

Scrambling to my feet, I noticed a dark glob of muck sliding down the outside of my hazmat suit. Ew. I wriggled, trying to get the suit off without help. Yes, I'd ripped out an arm. No, that didn't make it easy.

As I rumpled and crumpled the material, I heard whirring to the side. The side meant not the iris, so I didn't panic as much as I could have. I recognized the clunking rumble of robot treads as it approached.

With my head inside the hazmat suit, I couldn't see anything. Twisting and wiggling more didn't help. I needed more light.

Something solid bumped the backs of my legs. Another unknown thing touched the side of my arm holding up the hood. Servos whirred. I worked harder to find the hole and get out of the suit. My head popped through the ripped hole, letting me see the situation.

The robot held two arms extended. One tried to clamp a vise around my legs, and the other had caught my arm in the hood, maybe mistaking it for my head. If I worked this right, I could get it to think it had captured me without holding me.

I raised a foot so the vise would close around that instead of my legs and pulled the other free. At the same time, I swung the hood until it caught in the vise and withdrew my hand. Its servos stopped clamping when it had a loose grip on my foot and the suit.

The arms swung sideways so it could carry me horizontally. I grabbed the arm holding the hood so I wouldn't fall. Slung from robot arms, I hoped a door would open because I didn't see any way out.

As if in response to my wish, a door opened, flooding the room with white light. On the floor, several chunks of meat in gray versions of multiple colors lay scattered over the iris. Like they'd caught on the chute or the iris itself.

I'd fallen into a meat disposal chamber. Maybe for

corpses when someone didn't make it through the wormhole right, or when the robots accidentally killed a person instead of capturing them. Ew.

I would not throw up.

Cages made of black bars lined two walls of the new room. With the robot heading toward one, I slipped out of its grip and climbed through the hole in the hazmat suit. I leaped for freedom. The robot didn't act like it noticed, and nobody came running through the regular door in the other wall.

As I backed into a corner, hoping it didn't notice me a second time, the robot opened a cage and laid the hazmat suit inside it. The robot used enough care that I suspected they'd programmed it to recover anyone it detected as not dead. Interesting. Their corpse disposal routine included a failsafe.

The robot shut and locked the cage. I crouched, as still as I could manage. Ignoring me, the robot trundled back to the corpse room. The moment the door shut, I let go of a breath and straightened.

Based upon everything I'd seen so far, if the blue-skin aliens had enough people, someone would receive an alert and come soon to investigate the not-corpse their disposal failsafe robot had rescued. They'd find the hazmat suit and hopefully decide the robot had malfunctioned. I didn't have a lot of time to escape.

When I stepped in front of it, the regular door swished aside. The new room had gray, metal-like examination tables and all kinds of medical equipment, like tiny knives, needles, and gauze. My pockets had nothing but space coral bones and a folding putty knife. I'd given most of the tools I'd found to the guys. They had more pockets.

I tried not to disturb too much as I searched the room for anything useful. The moment I found a bag with a strap, I shifted my approach to how much I could take without revealing my pilfering at first glance. Everything I found in drawers that would fit went into the bag. Never mind what it did or how to use it. In a pinch, I could find a use for anything.

As soon as I'd stuffed the bag full, I checked the room. Until they searched the drawers, they wouldn't notice anything missing or out of place. Good.

Did I dare to rush out? No, I could hide in that cabinet. They wouldn't look inside it. Why bother? They'd assume I fled because that's what anyone would do.

The cabinet held things I transferred to the newly-empty drawers as fast as I could. Then I crammed my body inside and pulled the door closed. Within a few minutes, I heard the outer door swish open. Shoes padded across the room. The inner door opened. A voice sighed and muttered in the alien language.

Score another point for Emma's hazmat suit idea.

When the outer door opened and shut again, I waited until a count of twenty, listening for any signs another person had entered instead of the first one leaving. Nothing. I pushed open the cabinet door and tumbled out.

Now I needed a way to leave the room without cameras capturing me.

On second thought, I just needed another hiding place to dart into. Stepping up to the outer door, I focused on scanning the next area, not rushing through. As the door slid open, I crouched.

That kind of thinking saved me. Tables lined the next area, and I saw three pairs of legs sitting on chairs at them, two with their backs to me, and all at a table beyond the first pair. I hustled to get from the doorway to the closest table and hid under it.

One pair of legs stood and approached the door. The other two pairs stayed sitting. They talked to each other. I grasped the gist of their conversation. They'd noticed the door open, and the one guy got up to check it out. When he found nothing, they all laughed it off, dismissing it. With the robot bringing in a hazmat suit, maybe they thought the facility had issues with malfunctions.

This batch of aliens might've come expecting to find problems. The one alien we'd encountered prior to firing up the wormhole may have sent a request for help without an explanation.

Lightweight things clacked together. The aliens chatted. I spent several minutes trying to puzzle out the sounds. Once I caught the differences in their voices, I pinpointed someone talking with his mouth full.

These guys shared a meal.

They ate in a room next to a medical bay for prisoner examinations? And only two rooms away from a corpse disposal unit?

Maybe the room had some other official purpose, and they ate here for convenience. Yes, that made a lot more sense than putting a mess hall in this location.

To escape this room, I had to move three tables up without those guys seeing me. I could wait. Or I could take the chance. With luck, I could get past them. They had no reason to look in my direction.

Unless I made a noise. Unless I touched something and the movement attracted their attention. Unless any of a dozen things happened and they decided to look at exactly the wrong moment.

I waited.

CHAPTER 7

Time passed much slower than I wanted. These three aliens sat and chatted forever. They leaned back in their chairs and acted like they'd stay for hours. I poked my head to the side and saw two aliens from the side. They each held black tablets and poked at them while chatting with the third.

I took a chance and crab-walked to the next table, sticking close to the wall. Alien number one laughed at something and slapped his knee, turning his head away from me. His buddy slapped his back and ducked, also laughing. My heart pounded as I slipped under the table across from theirs.

To reach the next table, I had to pass one more alien.

Their laughter faded. One alien said something stern, and they shifted to huddle over the table. Something clunked on the surface.

If only I had one of those tablets. How could I get one?

Geez, Emma, don't aim for the moon or anything.

Still, if I could think of something, I wanted to do it. Did I have any options for getting all three of them to stop everything and rush elsewhere? No. Could I pickpocket something? Not without them noticing. A weapon would've helped a lot.

I had knives in my new bag. Using a knife to hurt someone didn't sit well with me. Ethan could kill. The other guys could too. They'd done it before and would do it again. Marines trained to do that sort of thing.

Imagining my big brother killing someone made me ill.

Never mind. I had no intention of killing anyone. Knives could cut things besides flesh, and that was how I planned to use them.

Other things in my bag might have uses at the moment. Moving slow to stay quiet, I opened the flap and checked inside the bag. Digging for anything would make noise, so I could only use stuff on the top.

Scalpel, gauze, tape, scissors, things I had no names for. Since I knew I had multiple scalpels, I plucked that from my bag. Not to cut any of the aliens.

With all the strength I could muster while hiding beneath a table, and a healthy dose of desperation, I chucked it back toward the medical room. The tool clanged off a table leg and winged across the room into the corner opposite me. Thank goodness.

All three guys jumped to their feet. They rushed to that end of the room. As soon as they passed, I rushed across the aisle and under their table. Groping upward, onto the surface, I found a tablet and swiped it.

And I thought my heart had hammered before. My pulse thundered in my ears. I dove to the next table and across the aisle again. Any moment, they'd check under the tables and discover me.

One crouched in the corner and picked up the scalpel. The other two rushed into the medical room.

I ran at the door and slipped out. Maybe the one guy saw me, and maybe he didn't. Either way, he had to have noticed the door opening.

Outside the door, I discovered a narrow corridor. How long did I have before alien number three checked the door? Ten seconds or so, probably.

This corridor had another door across the way. Never

mind caution. I scampered to the other door and plunged through it.

Light flickered on for me, revealing a small locker room. No one was inside it except me. For the moment, I'd found a safe hiding place. I examined my unlikely prize and wondered if they had GPS locators, or something like them.

If they could find the tablet, I could probably use it for five minutes before I needed to ditch it and my hideout. Alien guy would search the immediate room first, thinking he might've dropped it and kicked it. At least, I hoped he would. That's what I would do.

I tapped it and scanned the screen. Alien writing covered it with bubbles around four sections. I picked one. The bubble turned green.

The aliens took tests? You're welcome, alien guy, for my accidentally getting that answer correct.

As with other screens here, tapping the upper right corner shrank the immediate image in favor of a menu with a dozen choices. Looking them over, I didn't recognize any of the glyph sequences, though I did recognize some of the glyphs themselves. This tablet didn't help me.

I picked a random locker and dumped the tablet inside it. Good thing I'd taken that chance and deprived myself of a hiding spot for no reason. Go me.

Nothing for it but to find another door. Opening the door was a risk, staying was a risk. Breathing was a risk, or so it seemed.

The door slid open when I crouched in front of it. Down the hallway, an alien leaned around the corner, looking down a different corridor. I ran at full speed in the other direction. The next door I saw, I ducked inside.

Six robots sat in square charging docks, lights over them flashing red. Each docking station hung from a pair of treads on the wall to lift or lower the robot in question. Above each robot, seams marked a door the same size as the docking station base.

Not sure where to go, I climbed a robot to investigate the doors. Pushing on it accomplished nothing. I patted the wall all around the robot. Then my idiot self found a button on the floor of the docking station. The aliens wouldn't want to ride up the elevator or get clipped by robot arms, so they'd put the button on the floor. No one would catch a ride by accident.

I slipped down and stepped on the button, then hopped onto the robot. Motors whirred and clunked. The platform lifted. Overhead, the door opened. We ascended through a square column the right size for the robot.

When the platform stopped, a door in front of us opened. I jumped out. The robot stayed inert.

Stumbling into yet another corridor, I oriented as fast as I could. Narrow corridor. Bright lights. Doors. Like the rest of this stupid facility.

Wait. I knew this corridor. I'd rescued the guys from that room with the blood spatter on the door. Baldwin had stabbed an alien in the hand with an improvised screwdriver, causing it to bleed. These doors locked on the outside. With the things inside my bag and enough desperation, I could open a deadbolt from the inside.

Summoning that much desperation didn't seem like a challenge. I dashed through the door with the blood and shut it behind me. The empty room glowed with dim red light. For the moment, I had safety. As long as the camera hadn't noticed me.

Crap. That run had taken too long.

I couldn't handle much more of this without a break. But I had to. One more dash to the next cell down should earn me a reprieve.

Deep breath in. Hold. Deep breath out. Repeat. Open door. Check in both directions.

With the corridor clear, I ran like a feral bear chased me. At the next door down, I flung it open and dove inside.

Shut the door. Breathe. More breathing. Holy crap, did

I need to breathe.

My body ached from all the panic, running, and contorting. The situation crashed around me as I realized I had no idea how to find Ethan and the guys. For all I knew, they lay dead in that robot room because the aliens had decided to cut their losses. Robots would drag them to that chute, then the iris would open and swallow them all.

Ever helpful, my brain supplied a vision of a room where bodies fell into a boiling vat of corpse stew. The aliens cooked dead people and used them as material to make their weird space coral alloys.

No, brain, they probably dumped the corpses into space. Rendering bodies required too much effort to get no benefit. They'd have to melt all the fats and dehydrate everything, then pulverize the bones and mix all the powder together. Adding that to metal, at least, didn't improve it.

Ugh, why did I even know that? I'd read an article about a guy who'd done it with his dead aunt to see what would happen. The article had appeared in an engineering journal because he'd tried to use the resulting alloy to build an engine for a DIY scooter. The engine hadn't achieved standard engine performance metrics on the first test, then it blew on the second.

His conclusion? Don't do it. Dispose of bodies properly.

Stop thinking about corpses, Emma. They hadn't killed Ethan and the guys. End of statement. This was no time for crying.

Burning built in my eyes anyway. I slid to the floor and hugged my knees. With my back to the wall beside the door, I couldn't hold it back any longer.

I cried because I'd worn myself to nothing.

CHAPTER 8

No one came for me while I wept into my knees. I knew the rooms had cameras, yet nobody monitored this one. Maybe the cameras on the prison rooms operated all the time, not when they detected motion. If so, someone had to know to check the feed for this specific cell for them to see me.

At some point, I wiped my face and ignored the rumble in my belly. I stood and checked the door. It still opened freely. They hadn't discovered me and tried to lock me in. No one monitored the camera inside this room. I could do anything I wanted in real safety.

Safe and unnoticed, I sat again and emptied my bag to inventory the contents. To avoid noise, I plucked each item with care and laid it on the floor, arranging everything in groups. By the time I finished, I had five groups.

For the blades, I had three scalpels, two pairs of scissors, and one tiny set of clippers. One syringe sat with a spool of thread, a small plastic square the size of my thumbnail with a circular symbol stamped on it, and a magnifying glass as a group of things unlike the rest. Two wads of gauze made up the soft and fluffy group. The tweezers group had three pairs of different sizes.

The last group had a dozen small round discs of soft material with smaller hard plastic discs in the center. They reminded me of the dots doctors put onto patients to monitor their heart rate or pulse. As far as I knew, those dots needed wires to work. These dots didn't have wires or a place to connect wires.

If these dots did the same thing, they either had tiny batteries or a way to pull current from a body somehow. Anything generating a current could potentially help me, no matter how it worked. Since I had twelve, I picked up a dot and used a scalpel and tweezers to dissect it with the aid of the magnifying glass. My knees provided a way to hold something, giving me a third hand of sorts.

I missed my model-building tools at home. The setup I'd used to construct a custom model from an array of parts made my current situation look like a pathetic joke.

As I pried off the plastic dot in the center, I tried to think of anything else I missed about home. Nothing.

Okay, not nothing. I did miss the part where I didn't have to run to evade aliens and cameras. Except I had to evade hands and fat. So far, I hadn't figured out how to do either. Or how to get out of Dad's dream for me to become an accountant.

How did he think I'd ever do well at that? Sure, I managed my best grades in math, but only because I'd worked hard to learn calculus on my own. High school algebra hadn't taken any effort when I already understood derivatives and integrals.

Daddy's little girl would follow in his footsteps because Daddy's little boy had rebelled and joined the Marines. Go to Bentley and become an accountant or else. Ethan had picked the "or else" part. Despite wanting to, I hadn't.

I forced myself to breathe, hoping it would chase away the clutter in my head. Dad, Bentley, failure, food, fat, my ugly self, Andy…ugh, I really didn't want to think about Andy. Or any of the other boys I'd dated since Ethan had enlisted.

Why did I even go out with any of those boys? I didn't know. Around then, I'd started noticing all the fat hanging off my body. People called me pretty, but I never saw it in the mirror. They all lied to me, mocking me. Like the whole world had colluded to prop me up so they could laugh at me behind my back.

Thank goodness I hadn't swiped a mirror in all this stuff.

The plastic disc popped in half. Tiny pegs holding it together also held the soft ring in place. I removed the soft ring and examined the internals. The tiny nubs and dots reminded me of circuitry, which I understood. These parts didn't correspond directly to what I knew, but I could follow the pathing.

If this tiny thing acted as a switch, then that tiny thing produced the charge. I tried prodding it with the tweezers and nothing happened. When I touched the spot with my finger instead, it zapped me with a jolt so teensy I barely felt it.

The dot used the conductivity of flesh to close the circuit. Assuming it provided similar function to the dots I knew from watching a few episodes of medical dramas, this other part acted as an antenna to transmit the data it collected to a nearby receiver.

Using this might prove more challenging than I thought. But at least I had some things to think about. More knowledge about how the aliens designed and built tech helped, even if I couldn't see how.

I spent a few minutes repacking my bag. To get out of the room, I either had to run from door to door or find a way to interrupt or otherwise block or disrupt a camera.

Where would I go when I left? Time to list my objectives and prioritize them. One, find the guys. Two, reunite with the guys. Three, signal Akata. Four, get off the facility and onto Akata. Number three still hit highest on that list.

Ethan had probably freaked out within five seconds of discovering he'd lost me. By now, hours later, he must've reached the point of assuming the aliens had caught me. He couldn't have evaded capture himself, not for this long. Those guys had too much drive to press forward and rush into rooms without knowing their contents.

Side note—my stomach growled. I ignored it.

Figuring the guys sat in a room like this one, I could knock them down on the priority list. After all, they had no clue how to find anything relating to sending signals or manipulating lights. Whenever I found that, I wouldn't need them for anything other than lookout duty.

As such, my immediate problem had more to do with knowing what to look for than anything else. I checked the wall. Like most of the facility, panels covered it. These people had already proved they didn't have a proper appreciation for fasteners, so the lack of screws or rivets didn't surprise me.

Folding putty knife in one hand and scissors in the other, I attacked a seam between panels. They used some kind of rubbery gray material that matched the color of the walls. The putty knife cut the stuff with an application of elbow grease. By the time I'd cut through a strip of sealant about twelve inches long, I needed to stop and catch my breath.

I jammed the scissors in for more leverage. Opening the blades took all the strength my hands had. In return, I made more progress in a shorter time and with less work. Once I had the side open, I scraped the scissors blade across the top. That let me rip off the entire panel.

Behold, the inner guts of the wall. My panel had covered a four foot square. Inside, vertical beams about half an inch thick provided a shell at two-foot intervals. For an interior wall with no expectation of load-bearing, that seemed sparse, except they had stronger, weirder materials than we did on Earth.

On the left, the support beam formed one side of the door frame. Each support beam also held a narrow rectangle as part of its structure at two feet up, forming a vent or pipe through the wall. At the door, it turned downward to dip under the floor, and probably re-emerge on the other side.

The vent radiated heat, so I guessed it had involvement

in the life support systems, either for air or water. I tapped the vent with my scissors. It sounded hollow.

This vent helped keep the station warm enough for people. Could I use that to my advantage? Not at the moment. Stabbing a hole in it would warm up the room, but at what cost? If the aliens had caught the guys and stuck them in a different room, I might cut off their heat.

No stabbing the vent so long as I had to stay on the station.

Between the rightmost pair of struts, I noticed a strip of black goo that I'd already learned carried electrical wires. The goo hugged the outer wall. I stuck my head in as far as I could and saw the goo curling under the floor. It also ran upward.

I might've found the camera wiring.

This wall kept going past the floor, though I didn't have enough light to see far into it. The wall also continued upward. My body wouldn't fit into the gap, so I couldn't crawl around the facility innards from here. If I had a reason to, though, I could run wire or thread up or down. Left or right didn't seem feasible because the beams didn't have holes other than the vent.

Wanting to see the camera itself and confirm I'd found one, I pried off the upper panel. The black strip of goo split and entered two small, square devices. One had a tiny round lens.

I'd found a camera! Maybe two of them! This stupid, small discovery gave me a huge thrill of victory. Not only had I discovered a thing, I'd correctly predicted where to find it. With one camera offline, I could gain a tiny sliver of freedom to roam.

Taking it apart would give me tons of insight into how the aliens did things because I already knew how a camera worked. I knew how a motion sensor worked too. Everything inside that box should make sense to me.

With either of those things in hand, I could have a

primer on alien technology. I only had to get it off the wall where it hung eight feet up, otherwise known as two and a half feet over my head.

Sure. No problem.

CHAPTER 9

I stared at the cameras for a while, trying to imagine how to get them off the wall. In addition to reaching up there, I had to cut the wires and also remove the boxes from the wall. At least they didn't use screws or rivets, but I wouldn't have much leverage below it.

The guys would've just hefted me up there with their big, beefy arms. I could've sat on Ethan's shoulders. Hedy Lamarr would've done that, along with delivering some witty comments about it.

Which didn't help me in the slightest. By myself, I had to get my hands up there. And I had to have the use of both hands.

From a few steps back, I surveyed the situation. The panels wouldn't help me. Cutting or bending them required serious tools or muscles, or both. A four-foot panel wouldn't fit into a two-foot gap in a useful way.

If it would hold my weight, I could stand on the vent and brace between the two support beams. I might need more elevation, or I might not.

I returned to the open wall and gave each surface, including the vent, a good test with my hand. Everything remained steady and in place. The four-inch-wide beams had nothing I could hook the soles of my boots on to climb them. This also meant they had nothing to tear up my hands or other fleshy parts.

Emma Peel, my other hero, would wedge herself between two surfaces to climb up. In her catsuit. She'd scale up there in no time, swipe a fancy letter opener across the sealant to cut it apart, and jump down with a flip and a flourish, holding one camera in each open palm to present to Mr. Steed.

This Emma wouldn't manage the grace and elegance part, but I could put my back against one beam and my knee against the other. My second knee could act as a brace on the outside so I didn't fall into the room.

A few experimental shoves downward didn't dislodge the vent. The material didn't bend or bow. I took a moment to arrange the contents of my bag so I could reach in blind and not slice my fingers or grab the wrong thing.

Gripping the support beams, I set one boot on the vent. This would work. I bounced off the other foot and watched the vent. The material felt like it flexed under my foot, though I didn't see anything. Landing on the floor again, I stepped down and inspected the vent for any visible stress fractures or other obvious issues.

As far as I could tell, the vent would hold. I set my boot on it again and bounced again. This time, I planted my second foot on the vent. The vent didn't feel completely stable. I thought it wobbled a smidge. Maybe I imagined it?

If I fell, at least I had gauze to bandage myself. Unless I hit my head or something. Gosh, because nothing like that could ever happen.

Snorting at myself, I reached for the box to gauge the distance. Five and a half feet plus two feet put the bottoms of the boxes a few inches over my head.

I didn't trust the vent. With my back against one beam and my knee against the other, I pushed outward. This took my weight off the vent and gave me an extra two things to think about. For safety, I left my other boot resting on the vent. Just in case.

For a moment, I debated between the putty knife or a scalpel. The putty knife seemed too big for the job, so I used the scalpel instead. The work of cutting the boxes free took a lot more out of me than I expected. Shoving the scalpel upward, against the wall, was hard. I banged my knuckles fifty thousand times. The butt end of the scalpel pressed against my flesh, threatening to puncture it. My shoulder hurt.

Umpteen million times, my hands started turning numb. I had to leave the scalpel wedged into the sealant and let my arms dangle. The fifth time, I stepped down to give my shoulders and knee a rest. Marching around the room, swinging my arms, helped.

Then I climbed back up there and tried more. I wished I had that drill I'd given to Mendez. Or anything to help make this easier on my hands. Even that stupid tablet, because I could've used it as a makeshift hammer.

The scalpel finally cut through. My hand hurt so much that I dropped the stupid knife. It fell into the darkness below and clanged off the sides of the wall gap. I stumbled to the floor and sat. All excitement at the prospect of having those stupid cameras had died in the face of this challenge.

Ready to give up, I rubbed my hands and stared at the open wall.

If I didn't get a camera now, I doubted I'd find another chance this good later. How many alien devices could this station have that I would immediately understand? Maybe I could take apart a tablet or some other screen, but I doubted it would help as much. In another room somewhere else, I'd have to pry the wall open again and hope I picked a section with a camera.

No, I wouldn't give up. I only wanted to.

My stomach had stopped rumbling, at least. I'd crossed into the zone of too hungry to feel it anymore. Thank goodness I'd eaten that gross green bar, or this would've happened hours ago.

Did I just choose gratitude for having food with fat in

it?

Yes. Yes, I did. Weird. And good? A good kind of weird, maybe.

Bolstered by that, I stood and fetched a second scalpel. The stupid cameras now represented something. If I could get one or both, I'd take a big step forward in the quest to get off this stupid space station. No more blundering with screens.

Okay, not true. I'd still have to blunder with screens. But at least I'd have a better chance of finding the wiring to send a signal to Akata.

I took a deep breath, hopped onto the vent, and attacked the sealant around the cameras again. Once I'd made a hole big enough, I wedged the scissors in and used it as a lever to make cutting the rest of the sealant easier. Actual progress happened.

At some point, maybe ten minutes later, I stepped down and shook out my whole body. My hands shook, my neck ached, and my knee hurt from pressing against the wall. But I would not give up.

I climbed up again and got more done.

An eternity later, both boxes popped off the wall together. I hacked through the wires with the scissors. Then I pulled them down with me and silently proclaimed victory by promptly lying on the floor and letting every muscle in my body relax.

Sitting up took a lot out of me. I leaned against the wall and waited for a spate of light dizziness to pass. My throat had never felt so dry.

I wished I'd grabbed food from those three aliens instead of a useless tablet. Even if they'd had cheesecake slathered in strawberry sauce, I would've rather eaten that and kept it down than eating nothing.

God, I missed real food. One week of noodle bowl and green bars, and whatever the other crap was, and I couldn't even remember how pizza tasted.

Stop thinking about food, Emma. You know how to do

this. It's not hard.

Picking up the boxes beside me, I focused my attention on them. Each box had one side sealed into place, so I cut both open with the putty knife. Inside, the blocky devices had three anchor points and three wires. The tiny clippers from my medical bay raid worked well on those.

Finally, I found screws again. These required the triangle tool, so thank goodness I'd found it. Without that, I would've had to try to wedge a scalpel in the tiny hole.

So far, I'd only seen screws in small things, like these cameras. Go figure. Their design methodology needed more logic. Not that I wanted to complain. Their insistence upon using the sealant for most things helped me.

I dissected the machines. One had more complexity than the other. The first box had one wire leading to the lens and a tiny silver nub. The rest of the housing held nothing and did nothing. They'd probably made a whole bunch of the same housing and used them for whatever worked. That kind of thinking saved money.

It occurred to me that the sealant might cost less than lots of screws or rivets. Akata could provide blood coral bones, like the ones in my pocket, practically on command. If the aliens had similar colonies of the gray coral base of the sealant, that might explain their reliance on it.

On the side of the second housing, I found a simple switch connected to a tiny box with a connection to all three wires. A motion detector closed the circuit to activate the camera and microphone. Therefore, the tiny box housed the motion detector. One thick cable ran between the motion detector and the lens and microphone.

As I'd suspected, the cameras inside the cells didn't have motion detectors. The ones in the hallways did.

Some time later, I had both devices disassembled as much as possible. I'd learned a ton more about how the aliens designed their tech.

They favored simplicity, squares, and straight lines. In

some cases, they hadn't bothered to advance their designs past the basic, like the switches. In others, they'd created elegant works of art. The camera devices specifically used a streamlined approach only possible through processes I couldn't imagine.

At this point, I felt I had a basic, rudimentary idea of how they did things from an engineering and design point of view. Faced with a small-scale device, I could figure out how it worked and what it did.

Knowing what the space station did, and generally how it worked, I thought I could make some good guesses about the stupid, weird design.

I knew it had the ability to send signals. With the long, tubular shape of the station, and the spinning rings surrounding it, I thought I'd put the communications antennas on the ends. Putting them on towers would provide maximum coverage in every direction.

My next stop? One end or the other. Without letting any cameras catch me, running into any aliens, or passing out from extreme hunger.

Challenge accepted.

CHAPTER 10

I packed the pieces of the cameras, without the screws, into my bag. The housings wouldn't fit, but everything else did. When I stood, my vision clouded with a hint of static. That hadn't happened to me in a week or so.

Now that I knew I had a problem, I had a thought on the cause of the static. For over a year, I'd had spells where my vision had clouded over with fuzzy black and white spots, like when the cable TV signal fails. Once, it had happened while driving and almost killed me. Usually, it happened when I stood up or made other sudden, full-body movements.

Though it pained me to admit it, I had a feeling I'd starved myself. Ethan had called me gaunt. My friends had joked about seeing my bones and needing to put more meat on them. No matter what I did, I looked in the mirror and saw a freakish fat girl, so I didn't understand any of it.

Starving myself presumably meant I'd failed to get all the essential things I needed from food. How could I get those things without bloating like a balloon? I had no idea. Maybe Akata could help me between the five zillion other things I wanted her to do.

In the meantime, I needed some food and water. I'd witnessed the aliens eating, so I knew they did it. Whether they ate food that worked with human anatomy, I had no idea, but I suspected they kept some kind of nutrition suitable for any organic life form. After all, they dialed their wormhole to access at least a dozen different planets and abducted people. Not keeping those people fed and watered would make the whole effort a stupid waste.

If I had to keep food for prisoners, I would keep it near the prisoners. Robots would deliver it to reduce the chances of escape. The doors opened outward to protect the hinges. How did they do it without anyone getting loose?

The robots had plenty of arms, so they probably opened the door wide enough to deliver the food, braced it with their bodies, and shoved the food inside. I imagined how the robots would maneuver and found this reasonable. Anyone venturing too close would get zapped. That batch of prisoners would learn their lesson and not try to escape.

Wait. How did they get the prisoners from these rooms to the ships they used to deliver them elsewhere? Ethan had talked about a confusing memory of acquiring rifles and getting dumped onto a ship with a different kind of alien. They'd battled the other aliens because they'd had no choice.

Getting their prisoners from this room to that ship, though, seemed like it lacked efficiency. These aliens liked efficiency. They could've zapped everyone and dragged them, but I didn't think so.

What if they had some other method to get food into the rooms? What if these cells all backed on a series of docking rings, or a hallway with no other exit except a docking ring?

My attention turned to the panels behind me. They looked the same as the rest. Two pairs of four-foot squares sat side-by-side. The back wall didn't have an angle like I thought a near-outer wall would. With the size of the station, maybe only the absolute outer hull needed a curve.

Putting the heating vent in the inner wall suggested it made more sense there than on the outer wall. Why put the heating vent where it had to go around the doors? Heat rises, and fleshy beings need it. They could've put the vents in the floor. Maybe they had something else running under the floor, or the supports couldn't accommodate it properly like a non-load-bearing wall could.

I attacked the left panel of the rear wall. My muscles ached, but I could handle cutting downward. When I ripped the panel loose, I discovered support beams, no vents, and a latch. Unlike the other wall, this one didn't have a view into the wall below. The wall ended at the floor. Checking upward, I discovered it also ended at the ceiling, and at both sides.

The latch had a black goo wire running across the outer panel, parallel to the floor, and through a series of small holes in each support beam. At the side wall, it turned and ran up to the ceiling, where it disappeared through another hole to the side.

This back wall swung open like a door, activated by some remote means. I couldn't see the hinges, but I knew it had to work that way.

Instead of trying to make the door work, I cut the wire to the latch, then worked on cutting out the outside panel. An outer hull would have a lot more protection than this, so I knew I'd find a hallway or another room beyond it.

As dumb as I thought avoiding screws was, the aliens didn't set up anything truly stupid. Storing prisoners you wanted to use someplace where you might accidentally space them with the wrong lever or button push counted as truly stupid. Therefore, they hadn't done it.

Removing the outer panel took less effort than the inner ones had because I could kick it. The panel fell into a wide, dark corridor with a muffled thud.

Voilà! Behold my predictive brilliance!

Dim red light from the room spilled into the corridor. It ran left and right. Beyond the fallen panel, reflective red strips with arrow shapes pointing to the right ran along the middle of the corridor. I ducked through the hole and suspected I'd found a way to move at least a short distance out of sight of the cameras.

No, strike that. This hallway definitely had cameras. They'd want to watch. But like the prisoner rooms, they had no reason to use motion sensors here. When they had captives in need of transport, they'd actively monitor the corridor. Otherwise, ignore it.

The reflective strips glimmered in the dim light, stretching in both directions. I jogged to the left and found a pair of inert robots in docking stations. Green lights glowed above them, which helped me see. Beside them, a shelving unit held at least three dozen backpacks with contents. My presence and movement didn't activate the robots, so I judged the area safe enough for exploration.

Picking up a backpack, I found the weight manageable. For good measure, I took two and returned to the prison room to inspect them where I had meager light instead of a glow only bright enough to keep me from running into walls.

I emptied one pack with the same care I'd used for my bag and discovered a treasure trove. A gray coral canteen held fresh, clean water. Six packages wrapped in thin, papery material held bars similar to the green one I'd eaten earlier. A clip with a spring held a rectangular sheet of gray, rustling material large enough to cover Ethan's big, muscle-bound body.

Gnawing on a block of food, I refolded the sheet. Though the sheet had a lot in common with a mylar emergency blanket, it didn't fight my efforts and did accept the clip without issue. The food tasted like plain yogurt and had the consistency of a granola bar.

With every chewy bite, I reminded myself that my body needed food. Without food, it did not function properly. Engines needed fuel. My body was an engine. Food equaled fuel. I would eat. Hunger required feeding.

That last thing bothered me. The idea of feeding made it sound so animal and bingey. I tried not to think about it. Instead, I ran my fingers over the backpack. The smooth, dull material reminded me of satin without the sheen.

The aliens gave their prisoners these backpacks as they sent them to fight? Why not keep supplies on the transports? Why hadn't Ethan mentioned a backpack? Maybe he'd forgotten. After two years of watching friends die and fighting for his life, the little details probably didn't matter so much.

Maybe I needed to grab another two backpacks for the guys.

Then again, if the aliens had captured them, wouldn't I find them in one of the cells along this row? Unless they had some other place to store prisoners, I thought I would. The aliens would monitor the camera on them, so I needed to do something clever to find the right one and free them.

Okay, Emma. Time to get clever.

I waited for a brilliant idea.

And waited.

Then I sighed. If I opened the doors from the outside, the other cameras in the hall would catch me. If I knocked from the back corridor, the cameras in their cell would notice them responding. Once they knew I'd found a way to use the back corridor to my benefit, the aliens might decide to space us all through the docking collar I knew I'd find in that back corridor.

Once I knew which room held the guys, I could work on a real idea. I needed more information, or a way to contact them without making them act like idiots. And I had nothing.

All this work, and I'd only expanded the size of my prison. Way to go, Emma. Bravo.

I sat on the floor and stuffed my stupid food bar down my stupid throat, trying not to think about the stupid fat in it.

CHAPTER 11

Maybe ten minutes later, as I screwed the cap onto the canteen to stow it, I noticed the floor and ceiling also had panels. Duh. Putty knife and scissors, meet floor panel sealant. A match made in heaven!

Prying up the floor panel took more effort than the others had because I didn't have gravity in my favor. At least I didn't have gross hunger and dying thirst working against me anymore. My belly did kind of rumble still, but I thought it should have a chance to work on what I'd eaten.

I would eat enough food.

Later.

Groaning from the strain, I heaved the panel aside to see what lay beneath it.

Three more support beams, these much thicker and wider, ran from the front to the back of the room and beyond. One gap had black goo wires running through it. My body might fit in the space between the other two, if I stayed on my side. It had enough depth, at least. Whether the panel below would hold my weight, I had no idea.

If I fell at any point, I didn't want to leave any of my treasures behind. I lowered my two backpacks into the gap. Then I lowered myself into the gap with the other bag slung across my body.

Yes, I fit. Barely. These support beams, like the ones in

the wall, had no handholds of any kind, but they did have an I-shape. I hugged one beam with an arm and leg while I gradually shifted my weight to the panel.

The panel sagged a tiny amount under my weight. It also made a quiet creaking noise. But it held and didn't seem like it would break. Time to find out where this mad path would take me.

I wedged the backpacks between me and the beam. Using both forearms and both feet, I pushed myself sideways into the darkness. At the gap for the wall, the backpacks proved the only challenge. Looping my arms through the straps and taking my time got me safely past the chasm too narrow for my body.

The possibility of banging my head on something unseen worried me. More importantly, though, I didn't know how I'd get out of this tunnel. As soon as I had that thought, I paused and ran my fingers over the surface above me. No seam. Yikes. A few wriggles further, I found a seam running perpendicular to my direction. Panic averted.

My worries came true as I bumped my head against something. It didn't hurt, which I counted as a win. Once I wriggled my arms past my head, I groped a strange shape. Wires. A thick bundle of wires strung laterally across the gap blocked my path.

If I had structural gaps like this, I'd use it for wires too. Once I found this bundle, I was surprised I hadn't found more. On the other hand, they used the black goo method for everything else I'd discovered so far.

Whatever. These aliens made no sense to me. When I built my space station, I'd block this kind of access with vents and wires all over the place.

I pushed my two backpacks ahead of me, then shimmied under the wires on my back. Once I passed it, I had to take a break to breathe. As soon as I could, I started again and kept moving.

Crossing the station this way took forever. I wiggled

over wall gaps and under more wire bundles. Every once in a while, I checked for seams. At some point, I made sure I could figure out how to move backward. A few times, I heard muffled voices.

Instead of reaching a dead end, I reached a wall gap too wide to inch across like a sideways worm. My body would fit inside it, so I switched to vertical. If I hit another barrier, I could either go sideways again or climb back up. With my feet braced against one side and my back against the other, I used my arms to keep my balance and hold the backpacks.

The vertical beams had oval gaps, like they'd planned to feed wires or extra supports through and never had. If I wanted to, I could climb through them and move sideways instead of vertically. The walls were solid, though.

I took my time walking down the walls into colder and colder air. As I descended, I passed four more floor gaps. How many levels had I tumbled down in that body disposal chute? How many levels did the station have? Finding out seemed like it would take longer than I wanted to spend on this facility.

Maybe fifteen feet past the final floor gap, my boot hit a surface. It made a solid, deep thump noise. Unable to see anything in the total darkness, I probed with my foot. The floor had a gentle arc to it, like the walls in that docking ring corridor. I found space to one side of the floor. Waving my boot back and forth, I hit another surface of the same kind.

The image in my head, combined with the plummeting temperature, led me to believe I'd discovered the outer hull. I'd reached the bottom of the station, relative to its internal gravity. My feet balanced on a piece of the outer frame. In no way did I want to try touching the outer hull. It could withstand space, so I knew it could support me, but they didn't heat the air here.

I already shivered. Without some kind of protection, I suspected I'd succumb to hypothermia long before I could climb out of the frozen wasteland beneath my feet.

Nope. Not going any closer. Boundary discovered, noted, and marked for avoidance.

Walking up the wall took a lot more work than climbing down. Too cold to sweat, I panted as I reached the gap where I'd shifted to the vertical descent. This skulking thing needed to end soon so I could sit and recover, and maybe eat another bar.

Ugh, another bar. No, Emma, not now. Moving now, eating later. More exercise meant more food allowed.

The wide gap, since it ran straight up and down, probably marked the middle of the station. The floor of the prisoner section was above the screens room. I didn't know by how many floors, but I remembered taking the stairs down to the docking corridor from the wormhole room. The docking corridor and the screens room were on the same level.

To reach the bottom of the station from the prisoner section, I'd passed four floor gaps. Math whirred in my head. Most likely, I'd find the docking corridor one level lower than the prisoner section. Which meant the prison floor was the dock ceiling.

Before we'd opened the wormhole, one alien had arrived in his ship and caused us all kinds of trouble. The guys had dealt with him, which probably meant they'd killed him and stashed his body someplace. Unless this second wave of aliens had taken his ship, it still waited for him in that docking corridor.

This new realization offered me two options. I could either try to find the room with the screens, or I could try to get access to that first alien's ship. To reach the screens room, I had to pass through a living area for station crew. For the docking corridor, I had to cross to the other side of the station and get out of the ceiling.

I knew the cameras covered at least part of the docking corridor. Once I tumbled out of the ceiling, I'd leave a panel on the floor for anyone to find.

Wait. Had I made a stupid error here?

The motion sensors had activated the cameras when the station had no crew members. When that first alien arrived, he would've left them on. Rather, he wouldn't have bothered to turn them off. If he didn't sit in that monitoring chair, it didn't matter if the motion sensors turned on a camera.

With a significant number of aliens on the station, which it seemed to now have, they wouldn't use the motion sensors anymore. The feeds would become useless. Thirty screens in that room meant once they had about thirty people authorized in the station, the motion sensors wouldn't add any value.

If they knew I still roamed free, they might leave the motion sensors running. Did I dare to bet they didn't know?

Could the guys have possibly evaded the aliens long enough to hide again?

No, of course not. They'd attracted too much attention by shooting a robot. My efforts had only delayed those two intercepting aliens. When I disappeared, had the aliens realized I must've fallen into the chute? Or had they thought a malfunctioning robot had distracted them before returning to its docking station?

So many ifs and maybes made me nervous about doing anything. But I had to do something.

The guys had much more practice making snap decisions. All my life, I'd bobbled along, shrugging and letting other people choose for me. Boys had decided what to do on dates. Friends had decided where to go and what to do there.

Had my dad chosen a future for me because he'd noticed?

Had he thought the engineering thing was just a phase or caused by a crush on some handsome astronaut?

Had he seen me more than I thought? And also less at the same time?

Did this matter? No. I might never see my dad again. Even if I returned home through the wormhole, I didn't have to go home. Neither did Ethan. We were both adults. Dad couldn't dictate anything other than how he spent his money.

Make a decision, Emma. Do something. Face the fear. Whatever happened, I'd deal with it or die trying.

I stuffed myself into the gap to cross the station to the docking corridor. Wriggling to the other side, I pushed all the thoughts out of my head.

Move both arms. Shift both feet. Push. Repeat. Over and over and over. Keep going. Don't stop. No giving up.

My stomach growled, insistent and annoying. Once I dropped through the ceiling, I'd have to keep moving until I found a safe space to hide. Stupid stomach.

Despite my plan not to stop, I stopped. I would eat and prevent my belly from giving me away. Imagine if my stomach had growled in that room with the three aliens! No matter how much I didn't want to eat, I would eat.

Getting another bar out of a backpack took bending my arms at weird angles and groping in the darkness. Once I found one, I stuffed it into my mouth. I chewed some of the paper. The piece in my mouth dissolved and tasted like salty chicken. The choice to wrap the bars in this stuff suddenly made a lot more sense. This paper offered an extra protein and electrolyte kicker.

These aliens thought through so many things so well, then made simple mistakes. Bad for them, good for me.

Time to break on through to the other side.

CHAPTER 12

With no ability to go left or right, I wriggled all the way to the dead end. By dead end, I mean where the panels stopped and the air became colder than I preferred. As with the bottom of the station, the side had an air cushion, probably bolstered with a complex series of cross braces. Beyond that, I expected to find the outer hull.

I cut through the last panel seam. The more sealant I broke, the more the panel bowed under my weight. By the time I'd cut as much as I could reach between the beams, I could fit my hand under the supports. This meant I could also fit the putty knife under them.

When I could reach the edge under the beam, I paused and listened. No footsteps, no voices, nothing. Good. I sawed around a corner. Instead of ripping out, the panel bent enough to let me slip through. Even better than I'd hoped for, because this meant I wouldn't leave a panel lying on the floor.

I ducked my head through and checked the situation. The dimly lit and deserted docking corridor ran in both directions. In one direction, I saw the shadows of the stairwell where Baldwin had stopped and turned us around. Beyond it, I would find the living quarters and the screens room.

Below me, I noticed a green light on a panel beside a large door. Two doors down in the other direction than the stairs, I saw another door with a green light.

Remembering what I'd seen before, I realized I'd emerged above the airlock for the first alien's ship. If I needed a sign to make a decision, I'd gotten it.

First I dropped my two backpacks through, then I swung around and let myself fall through, feet first. I slung the heavier of the two packs on my back and carried the lighter one.

Above, the panel drooped at the one corner. Someone approaching from the stairwell wouldn't notice it. From the other direction, they might if they started far enough away. Not that I could do anything about it.

The green light beside the door stuck out enough to guess it would depress like a button. How many options did anyone need for this situation? Two—open and close. One button could handle that. Checking the next door, I saw it had the same kind of green button, but not glowing. I pushed the button in front of me.

As expected, the docking door opened. It separated into four triangles that slid into the wall in each direction. Bright light spilled into the corridor. I stepped into a short airlock with no view of the space outside. The door to the ship stood open. Instead of dashing across, I turned around. Anyone stepping into the corridor would see the light from the open airlock. I needed to close it.

On the inside, the airlock had one red button. No sane designer would put a button to disengage the airlock inside the airlock. Not without a cover or some other mechanism to prevent accidental use.

Not that I considered the aliens completely sane. I did expect them to have a keen sense of self-preservation, though. After all, they used slaves to fight their battles.

I pushed the button.

Both doors whirred closed with that triangle design. Crap. My panic brain decided to dive into the ship. The door made a loud honk noise as I leaped through the closing portal.

Of course. People interested in self-preservation

included safety protocols on their outer doors.

Two seconds after I cleared it, the door resumed closing. A screen beside the door showed a view of the airlock. To my relief, it didn't disengage. As soon as I figured out how to open the door from this side—it didn't have a handy, obvious button—I could leave anytime. My button pressing hadn't irretrievably stranded me on a ship with all its instructions in an alien language.

As for the ship, it bore a strong resemblance to the station, except much, much smaller. I stood in a corridor wide enough for me to pass and tall enough for my hair to brush the ceiling. The hallway stretched about twenty feet in both directions, then ended at doors.

Yet another alien place to explore. I picked left. The ship had the feel of...a ship. Like an ocean vessel. Doors opened with a twist of a wheel. Everything was gray. No area, no matter how small, had wasted space. Rolled fabric and gray boxes hung from the low ceilings and on every wall.

The ship had two rooms with hammocks and closets, suggesting it could carry four at most, or maybe eight if they got cozy. In the engine room, I had to step over and duck under pipes to slip through the narrow passage. Equally narrow spaces allowed access to the sides of the engine.

I wanted to stay in the engine room long enough to understand how it worked. Maybe I had time for that, but probably not. The sooner I signaled Akata, the sooner she could help me formulate a real plan to assault the station and get the guys home.

No, I'd get us all home. I would go through that wormhole. Without Ethan, I didn't have much to live for, either here or at home. With him, I knew I could tackle anything. Like, for example, now. I'd crawled through the bowels of an enemy space station to reach an enemy ship.

Of course, I'd done that myself. No one had helped me pry off those panels. Ethan and his Marines wouldn't have fit through the space I'd squeezed into.

Yay me, but also, how in the heck would I get them out of the station without taking too many chances on the cameras? Maybe they wouldn't pick us up, or maybe they would. The aliens might even notice us by chance.

We needed a path straight to Akata from their cell.

Straight to a docking ring. Like through that corridor behind the cells.

Akata could cozy up to that and protect us while we leaped across. She'd done it with a different airlock, so she could to it with that one. Come to think of it, where had she docked before? No, it didn't matter. I needed to find a way to communicate exactly what I wanted to Akata, and a way to signal her when I had the guys ready and waiting to go.

Hopefully, I'd explain it well enough. She wouldn't be able to ask me questions. Which made no difference at all until I figured out how to send a message. I'd expected to do that from the station, but this ship might do the job instead.

If I could find the equipment and figure out how.

Predictably, I found the control room last. It had a similar shape and feel to the wheelhouse of a small boat without the actuality of one. Instead of gauges and obvious directional controls, screens covered the walls and a console area. Toggle switches and thick, clunky dials created dividers below each row of screens. In the front, above the console and where a window would otherwise offer a view outside, a large screen covered the entire wall.

This room inched me closer to my goal. I loved this room. Standing inside it gave me a rush of joy.

And I do mean standing, because it didn't have a chair or stool.

Since I knew these aliens had similar physiology to humans, I also knew this control room had minimal manual operation capabilities. No one would stand to operate a ship for long periods of time when the space had room for a chair. For short periods of time, a chair would get in the way. Besides, it had no obvious flight controllers.

Given the number of screens, I suspected they each had a dedicated function, or at least a primary one. Those under the viewscreen would affect navigation. Something capable of communication would have a microphone. After seeing the tiny mic with the camera I'd dissected, I didn't think I'd notice one.

A camera, though, I might have some luck finding. They used clear lenses made of glass-like material. If they did video conferencing between ships, this room ought to have a camera. None of the other rooms I'd seen suited the purpose better, as far as I could tell.

I ran my fingers over all the lines of toggle switches and dials, checking all the ones a few inches above eye level. Anyone who wanted to send a message would want to send their face, not their chest or lower. The aliens I'd seen so far all stood taller than me by at least an inch or two.

Funny how this ship had such a low ceiling.

Nestled between two toggle switches, I found a small lens at the height of my forehead. It sat below the middle screen on the back wall. The view it provided would include my head and the main viewscreen. That would allow the speaker to manipulate what the person on the other end saw in the background.

If I wanted to spend forever figuring out every function of this stupid control room, I could use that. Since I didn't, I figured I'd use the camera to show Akata my face. I wanted her to know I'd survived and hadn't used the wormhole, and this wasn't a trick by the aliens.

The screen above the camera flickered to life when I tapped it. With the camera below it, this screen seemed safe enough to poke at, so I poked. As with the other recent screens, I recognized some of the glyphs. This time, I recognized the one that turned audio on and off.

One screen appeared to ask me if I wanted to connect to the other alien ship, a few docks down. No, thank you. Then it showed an interesting image of a cone, possibly indicating my signal would blast in every direction. I wanted that.

Yes, the aliens would pick it up. They didn't speak English. Using this did mean they'd know about me loose on the station. That would've happened regardless of the method I used to send a message.

My next tap showed me the last thing I wanted to see. In the blue-white light of the room plus the screen, my face stared back at me. I blinked at the gross freak on the screen, half surprised and half disgusted.

Red curls sprang from my head in every direction. Otherwise, I couldn't pinpoint what looked so wrong. My nose didn't have any blackheads, and my forehead didn't have any pimples. Usually, my eyes appeared kind of dull and yellowish, but today, they didn't. In fact, considering all the crying I'd done lately, they looked really white and bright, and the blue seemed deeper than usual.

Maybe the digital image construction algorithms automatically corrected for blue to make the aliens easier to render. Did that explain the whites of my eyes or the pinker than usual undertones of my skin? Maybe? Colors aren't really my thing. I match stuff by picking things that don't take thought. Any color goes with itself and white or black.

Having to watch myself talk made this feel a thousand times harder. Would I have to listen to myself too? Ugh.

But if I could wriggle through the guts of a space station, I could listen to myself for two minutes. The toggle switch next to the lens probably turned it on and off. The dial on the other side likely controlled volume, or maybe signal strength. Not sure which end meant high or low, I left the dial alone.

After spending half a minute thinking about what to say, I took a deep breath, flipped the toggle, and stepped back so Akata would see my whole face.

"Akata, I hope you can receive this. It's Emma." I waved. For no reason. "In about an hour, we need you to pick us up from the station. There's a docking ring on the opposite side of the station as the two docked ships. We'll be there, waiting for you. If I can figure out how to do it, I'll turn on a light at the ring so you know we're there. Please come get us. We need your help."

I flicked off the switch. Time to hustle my butt back across the station, rescue the guys, and get us out of here.

No big deal.

CHAPTER 13

I ran to the airlock and smacked the green button. When it opened the door, I cheered on the inside. It could just as easily have disengaged the airlock. Then I would've had to figure out how to pilot the stupid ship.

On the other side of the airlock, I smacked that green button. Without waiting for the door to close, I ran up the empty corridor. At the stairs, I paused. Maybe thirty feet farther up the corridor, I'd find a crew area and a room full of screens monitoring all the station camera feeds. They'd have one showing the guys.

If I found it empty, I could make sure I'd find the guys before opening all the prisoner cells. I could smash all the screens to cause some chaos and prevent anyone from knowing where to look for us.

If someone sat in the room, or if anyone in the entire area noticed me, I'd get caught.

The potential benefit outweighed the risk of at least checking the area. I tiptoed to the open doorway and peeked around the corner. At the end of a hallway lined with doors, the door to the screens room stood open.

No one milled about, and I couldn't hear any voices. Something in the screens room moved. Could I pop my head inside, scan the screens, and leave without them noticing me? One way to find out. Moving along the wall, wondering why

I'd do something this insane, I paused at each open doorway and checked through it before darting past.

This area had dorm rooms, each set up for two people to live together. It also had a dining area and a group bathroom.

The aliens probably had to run diagnostics or patrol, so they had no reason to stay down here. Except for the guy in the screens room.

Why did they put a monitoring room with the living quarters? Did this station have more than one area with living quarters? How about a second or third screens room?

Geez, Emma, way to create problems. Like I needed more complications in the plan.

I reached the back wall, crouched to put my head low, and peered around the door frame. Someone inside hummed a tune similar to Twinkle, Twinkle Little Star. No one sat in the chair surrounded by a near-sphere of thirty screens. Instead, I saw a pair of black boots behind the screens.

Of course. I'd disabled more than half of the screens by ripping out the wires. For the rest, all the ones too high for me to get leverage for that, I'd removed the wires in a more polite fashion with a screwdriver. As I'd done that, I'd tangled up the wires as much as possible.

This poor schmuck had the job of fixing that mess. So far, he'd fixed one, and it showed the guys in a prison cell.

To think I'd spent so much time worrying about the cameras! This guy hadn't even started fixing them until maybe ten minutes ago. Or he might've set up the one right away and left the rest of the job until now.

Wait. No. I would not run rampant and carefree across the station. I had to assume they could monitor the cameras with some other device, maybe one that operated remotely. They had tablets, after all. Using one to access camera and microphone feeds wouldn't take much effort, so long as they had wireless capability.

Come to think of it, I wasn't sure they did have

anything like wifi on the station. Everything I'd seen used wires. That tablet I stole had three ports on the case, making it possible they loaded a program onto it, walked away and used the program, then plugged in to download the results.

How did they even get to the point of wormholes without wifi? By not caring if their devices could connect wirelessly or not. I didn't understand, but I didn't know much about their culture or society. At this point, I understood they didn't consider me as their equal because of my race, and they abducted people to fight battles for them. Also, they liked wide hallways and used the same design for toilets and showers as humans.

These people used different materials than us for almost everything. Maybe they didn't have the right raw materials to make the natural leap to wireless tech.

And maybe this didn't matter in the slightest, and I only thought about it because that beat dwelling on my problems.

Getting back to those problems, I needed to reach the guys and prep for Akata's arrival. The humming guy prevented me from accomplishing anything in the screens room, but at least I knew I didn't have to work so hard to stay hidden. Time to get moving.

I took a few soft steps away from the door to keep the humming guy from noticing me.

A high-pitched noise squealed for a moment, bouncing off the walls. Then a voice echoed from everywhere. I bolted for the docking corridor as an alien made an announcement over the PA system. At the doorway to the corridor, I stopped and peered around the edge. Two aliens with stun weapons stood guard at the airlock to the ship I'd broadcast from.

Another two aliens with stun weapons walked toward me, shining flashlight-style beams across the floor. They didn't sweep the lights upward, so they probably hadn't noticed the loose ceiling panel. Either that or they didn't associate it with me.

The announcement ended. I ran back into the living area and flew into a random dorm room. Shutting the door as softly as I could, I forced myself not to panic. Freaking out wouldn't solve anything or help me.

They knew they had a loose human on the station, as I'd expected them to realize. If they had some other way to monitor the screens, they'd use it to try to find me. I had to get stealthy as soon as possible.

The room had two beds, two desks, and two chairs, all metal. I tried lifting a chair and found it too heavy to move without scraping the floor. That much noise would bring the aliens running. And if I couldn't lift the chair, I definitely couldn't lift the other furniture.

Besides, I hadn't traveled far from the docking corridor. Beneath this level, I might find the station's outer hull instead of another floor. Why they'd put the living quarters so far from the center, I had no idea. The prisoner quarters kind of made sense, but for both, they wasted a lot of energy on heating.

These aliens had my respect for building a machine in space capable of generating a programmable wormhole, but a lot of their design decisions sucked.

My gaze snapped upward. The ceiling would take me back to the floor of the level where I wanted to go. I'd be in the wrong part, though, by about sixty feet or so. Except I could move in that direction at the center brace. But I had no way to know when I reached the right pair of beams.

Never mind. I'd worry about it when I got there. Moving laterally through the station's middle brace would take a lot of work, and I only had so much time.

Putty knife and scissors ready, I climbed onto one of the two beds. Because I'm not stupid, I picked the one with the ceiling corner out of sight of the door.

I managed to cut open the overhead panel through sheer determination and fear of discovery. My arms ached already, and this whole escapade had proved I needed to lift weights or something. Which meant I needed to eat more protein.

I recoiled from the idea of eating more anything. Just no. Never.

Maybe.

I'd think about it.

With two sides cut free, I had enough space to climb into the ceiling. If I could lift myself. Which I could not. Cutting the third side would make the loose panel too obvious in a casual check.

When I tried to put my weight onto the panel, it opened enough for me to see into the crawlspace. I would get my body up there. To underscore this, I tossed both backpacks onto the next panel toward the center line.

Take that, failure. I'd see you defeated because I needed to drink water.

Thinking about water made me thirsty.

As I gathered to jump, I noticed the bed had some bounce. This would work. I laid my hands on whatever I could, bounced a few times, then put everything I had into a jump.

My head whacked against the panel above and I fell onto the bed, cradling my skull. Way to go, Emma. I wanted to get up there so badly I'd jumped too hard.

The ache in my head faded to a mild throb as I rubbed it, and I didn't see any blood on my hand. I got up and tried again. This time, I didn't jump enough. After three more tries, I finally got enough of my body into that space without banging my head to get a grip on the ceiling. Using my feet on the walls, I wriggled my body into the gap.

I already knew how to carry the backpacks, and this part took nothing more than refusing to stop moving. Plus drinking water, which I did right away.

Onward to rescue my Marines.

CHAPTER 14

At the center brace, I moved into the wide gap and ducked to my right. By then, I had an idea. The floor ran flat. With the floor sitting on the support beams, I should only see light between the two pairs running to my prison cell. Even that dim red light would show up in the total darkness. Brighter light would shine in the other direction, through the gap in the docking corridor.

The chill didn't keep me from sweating this time. Squirming through the support beams took a lot out of me.

I emptied one canteen and dug into the second pack for another. Thank goodness I'd brought two packs.

Finding the right pair of beams after forever and a half of climbing came as a huge relief. Then I only had to wriggle on my side and slide under wire bundles for another forever.

Earlier, when I'd shimmied through without knowing how far I had to go, it hadn't seemed to take this long. With my goal in sight, I couldn't get there fast enough.

Finally, I reached the open floor and hauled myself out. God, I hurt so much. Every part of me ached. I lay on the floor, gasping for breath and too tired to keep going. My body didn't want to keep doing all this work.

"Marines first," I whispered to myself.

Easier said than done. First I rolled onto my side, then onto my hands and knees. My head swam. The ache pulsed with my heartbeat. All my limbs threatened rebellion.

"Tick tock." The aliens would start using the cameras as soon as they could. I had to move as soon as possible. The longer I delayed, the better equipped they'd get.

The crackle of the PA system jolted me to my feet. An alien voice shouted from everywhere. They sounded angry.

Motivated by adrenaline, I left my packs on the floor and cracked open the door to peer in both directions. No one stood guard in this hallway. Dumb on their part, but good for me. Leaving my door open, I jogged to the end and opened doors one by one. When I reached the cell next to mine, I found my four Marines.

Of course they'd sat in the next room all this time. Where else would they have put everyone?

Mendez leaped to his feet and half-tackled me into a hug. Ethan followed him.

"What—"

I laid a finger on my lips as Mendez squeezed me. "Microphones," I whispered. "Let go, Mendez."

He released me with a broad grin. Nash smiled at me. Baldwin stared with his mouth open.

"C'mon." I waved for them to follow me into the next room. We hurried.

They trooped inside behind me and all stumbled to a stop in a cluster.

"Holy crap, what did you do in here?" Ethan whispered. He pointed to the loose panels.

I shook my head. "Baldwin, shut the door, please."

He did it without complaint.

"There's a docking ring out there." I pointed to the back corridor. "Akata should show up soon."

Standing in the dim red glow of the cell, all four men stared at me like I'd told them I was the real Santa Claus.

"Why did you rip up those panels?" Ethan asked.

"How'd ya do it?" Nash lifted my arm and poked my scrawny muscles. "You got hidden superpowers or something?"

With a sigh, I picked up one of the backpacks on the floor. "If you want one of these, they're that way. The docking ring is in the other direction. I'm going down there."

"Why would we want one of those? What are they for?" Ethan took the pack from me like he meant to open it.

"Didn't you get one when you were herded through here?"

Nash moved into the corridor and crouched. He brushed his fingers over a reflective strip with an arrow. "I kinda vaguely remember being shuffled through here. It was pretty confusing, like they'd drugged us or used a mild stun or something."

"Yeah," Mendez said. "But we didn't get a pack. We got a rifle."

I hadn't seen any rifles. If not these guys, who did they give the packs to?

"We hit our first combat in maybe three hours," Ethan said as he poked through the pack. "Nobody gave us anything but the rifles. What is this?" He held up a paper-wrapped bar.

Weird. Did they have two classes of abductees? What did they use the other people for? How did they sort their prisoners?

Not that I wanted to find out today.

"Food," I said. "You eat the paper and everything. There's clean water in the canteens, and the other thing is a blanket."

"Baldwin, Nash," Ethan said, "run down there and grab two packs each. I don't know about the bars, but we can use canteens and emergency blankets. Meet us at the docking ring."

"Yes, Sergeant," Baldwin said. He and Nash jogged in the direction I'd indicated.

"Baldwin decided he wasn't really mad at you," Mendez whispered. "He was just mad." He smirked. "We had a lot of time to yell at each other. It's something we've practiced a lot, so we're good at it."

"Mendez, would you stop whispering to my sister," Ethan rumbled, his voice low and weary. The admonition carried no heat. He might've even found it funny.

I rolled my eyes. "I just rescued you. For the second time. I think I can decide who gets to whisper to me."

Mendez covered his mouth, and I thought he did it to smother a laugh.

Ethan draped an arm around my shoulders with a snort and guided me into the corridor. "What else did you do?"

I slid my arm around his waist, enjoying the company as we walked toward the docking ring. Spending all that time alone had made me a little battier than I'd thought. "I sent a message to Akata. I also freaked out a few aliens and disassembled a camera. And I discovered they haven't repaired all those screens yet. The guy fixing them isn't watching the feeds, so no one is paying attention. I'm pretty sure they know I'm running around, though. Those announcements over the loudspeakers were probably the guy in charge letting everyone know to watch for me."

"Chica, you're pretty amazing." Mendez took my hand and squeezed it. Then he let go. Like he didn't want me to think he expected any reciprocation or anything.

These guys. Looking back at how I lived day to day, I didn't think I would've survived much longer at home. Coming out here may have damned eight men to death and four to despair, but it had probably saved my life.

If only I could've found a way to get the help I needed without having to fall through a wormhole to the other side of the universe.

Baldwin and Nash rejoined us as we reached the docking ring, carrying four packs. They handed out packs so everybody carried one.

The docking ring had an iris instead of a four-triangle door. All four Marines would have to duck to get through it. I wouldn't.

"I don't suppose you managed to pick up any weapons?" Ethan asked.

I held up a scalpel. "Two of these, a putty knife, and pair of scissors is the best I've got."

Beside the docking ring, the wall had a screen. A button below it, like the other airlocks had, didn't glow. I tapped the screen. The display turned on and showed a view of the outside.

Thank you, screen, for doing exactly what I'd hoped for. Finally, something easy.

Ethan took the scalpel and examined it in the dim light. "If they're not watching the cameras, we could try for the wormhole again."

Baldwin grunted.

I held up the rest of my weapon-like tools.

"I dunno, boss." Mendez took the scissors and stuck the loops on his fingers. "I think we might be better off leaving, regrouping, and getting more weapons. They took almost everything we had."

"Mendez's got a point." Nash took the putty knife. He swished it through the air a few times like he needed to get the hang of it. "I'm as eager to get home as anybody, but not if we can make a better go for waiting a week. These aliens might even leave if we wait long enough. They did before."

Ethan nodded and glanced at Baldwin.

Baldwin sighed and took the last scalpel. "Waiting is smarter."

"Then we'll escape now and make a better plan with better weapons for a better assault." Ethan tousled my unruly curls.

On the screen, a small dot blocked stars as it moved. The dot grew. I nudged Ethan with an elbow and pointed. Akata had gotten my message.

Standing ready to smack the button I hoped opened the airlock, I watched. Our favorite lumpy, blood red spaceship neared the station at high speed. As she approached, she turned to the side to cover the airlock.

Two bolts of bluish-white light slammed into her hull. Akata hit the station hull and bounced. My heart stopped. Among the guys, I heard a colorful combination of curses.

"You didn't disable the station's weapons systems before calling her," Ethan whispered.

I gulped. "I forgot about them."

Another barrage of quiet yet heated curses filled the air around me. Akata drifted until another ship hit her with another beam of light. This one acted like a tractor beam. The ship pulled her out of sight.

I'd killed Akata.

CHAPTER 15

Ethan raked a hand through his hair and didn't look at me. "We need a Plan B."

I stared at the screen even though it no longer showed Akata. The other ship had towed her off screen. "I killed her," I whimpered. Then I covered my mouth, unable to breathe through my horror.

"Whatever we do, we gotta get outta here," Nash said. "They saw her coming, and they'll figure out right quick we planned to escape through this airlock."

"Cog." Ethan put his hands on my shoulders from behind. "It wasn't your fault." I heard the grind in his voice, like he didn't really believe that. He said it to make me do something. "We need to get moving."

Part of me wanted to let them go, push the button for the airlock, and join Akata where no one had to worry about anything ever again. Out there, I wouldn't have any guilt or pain. I'd pass out and never feel it.

Spacing didn't sound so bad when you understood how it worked.

Ethan squeezed my shoulders. "C'mon, Emma. Our next option is to make another run on the wormhole, and we need you for that."

Sure. I could open the wormhole for them, pretend like I'd follow, then shut it down and stay. They all wanted to go home so badly they wouldn't even notice me lagging. Maybe I'd even do my best to sabotage the device so the aliens couldn't abduct anyone else.

Turning away from the screen, I nodded. Ethan took my hand and pulled me along behind him. I didn't resist.

Knowing where to find the engines, I thought I could destroy the station. If I didn't escape before it blew, would anyone care? No. Especially not me.

We hustled into my ripped up prison cell.

Ethan let go. "Objective number one is weapons. Objective number two is the wormhole room. Objective number three is going home."

The other three guys chimed together, "Understood."

He nudged me.

I shrugged. "I don't want a weapon."

Between the guys, I caught a lot of slight head movements, like they used looks and nods to communicate. Everyone seemed to urge Baldwin to do something as far as I could see in the dim red glow.

Baldwin scowled and huffed. He stepped in front of me and crossed his arms. "Sorry I yelled at you," he mumbled. "Not your fault."

Ethan patted Baldwin on the shoulder. "Take point. Mendez—" He glanced between Mendez and me. Gears turned in his head. About something. I had no idea what. "Take rear. Nash, watch Emma. Let's move."

Had I missed something with Mendez? He seemed to find Ethan's choice funny. I found it weird.

Nash put a hand on my shoulder. He guided me out of the room behind Ethan. Mendez followed us. Checking back, I discovered him grinning at me like someone had told a good joke. Any other guy, I would've caught them staring at my ass. Except Nash hadn't when he'd taken rear earlier. Baldwin hadn't expressed any interest in my body at all.

We hurried through the hallway and I didn't have any more time for thinking about boys. Baldwin took us across the hall to an intersection. He stopped and peered around it. With a finger on his microphone button at his collar, he talked without making much noise or moving his lips. Ethan responded the same way.

Ethan waved at us. Nash herded me backward. Mendez slipped around us. The three men rushed around the corner while Nash and I stayed back. I heard grunting, a wet crack, and clattering. Someone howled for a moment before it cut off.

"Don't think about it," Nash murmured. "Or if you do, think about it as self-defense. We're done doing what they want and getting herded. Done."

Until he said something, I didn't think about it. Then I did. Those three men had their fists and the blades I'd given them. They wanted better weapons and a path to their objective. Marines would let nothing stop them from achieving their objectives.

I covered my mouth. Once again, I found a reason not to want to vomit. "They're killing those aliens," I whispered through my fingers.

Nash nodded. "Try not to look if it bothers you."

Try not to look. Close your eyes. Stop complaining. Nothing happened. Don't cry.

Turning away from him, I wished my brain would stop reminding me of things I wanted to forget.

"Hostiles down, let's go," Mendez said. "What's wrong with her?"

"Never seen death," Nash said.

These guys wouldn't understand. They couldn't understand.

One of them, probably Nash, touched my shoulder. I jumped. At least I had enough presence of mind to swallow the scream conjured by my worst memories.

Mendez slid in front of me. "Hey, chica." He touched a finger under my chin. "What if Akata was only stunned?"

"What?" He'd surprised me out of the past. I focused

on his face instead of that other boy's.

His mouth quirked into a faint smile. "I know you think you killed Akata, but what if she's only stunned?"

If the weapons had stunned her, she could bide her time after recovering and find a moment to escape. Akata might be fine. She could be okay.

I remembered something she'd said. "She told me she didn't know what the weapons would do to her."

"There you go." He pushed up on my chin, but gently enough that I could resist if I wanted. I didn't. "At some point, you have to stop beating yourself up over things you didn't remember or do and focus on the things you did. You forgot about the weapons. That's not really your fault. If we'd been there instead of locked up like dumb Marines, one of us would've thought of it. You're only one person, chica. You can't do everything. Nobody expects you to."

"I thought—"

"You thought of a whole lot more than anyone else." He wrapped his arms around me and held me close. "You did amazing. I never would've come up with ripping those panels off the wall. I don't even know how you got medical tools, and I bet we couldn't have found them. You figured out how to send a message to Akata. I guarantee none of us would've done that. You just also need a team. Everybody needs a team."

In his arms, I felt like someone cared. Of course, Ethan cared, but with Mendez, it was different. He had no reason to care, and yet, he did. I wanted to spill all my dark secrets to him, to tell him everything.

"This…this thing happened." I sniffled and forced myself to press onward. "A while ago."

He squeezed me tighter. "And I want to hear all about it. But not right this minute, okay? We're kind of in the middle of storming the citadel here, and that's not a good time for picking at old wounds. I promise I'll listen when we're safe."

Right. What was I thinking? I wiped my eyes. The

aliens would come for us any minute, and now we had dead bodies on the floor.

"They're stowed," Nash whispered.

I felt Mendez nod. "We're going to the wormhole room. You're going to make it work. We'll go home. Then you can tell me all of it. Okay, chica? As soon as we're safe and on stable ground, I'll listen. I promise."

He heard me and wanted to listen.

"Okay."

He kissed my forehead. I turned to face reality. Nash stood at the corner, keeping watch. These guys wanted to help me, not hurt me. Leaving them would hurt as much as going home. Maybe more. If they all went home, I could go with them. Why had I even thought the airlock made a good choice?

Never mind. We had a wormhole device to reach. With Mendez at my back, I put one foot in front of the other. I turned the corner. Baldwin waited at the next intersection, keeping watch like Nash. Ethan paced until he saw me. Had he wanted to come check on me, then let Mendez talk him out of it? He never stood around and let other people solve his problems.

Ethan saw me and sighed with relief. He took a step toward me, then hesitated with strangely non-Ethan-like uncertainty.

I didn't want to hold us up anymore. Flashing him the kind of smile most people would call "brave," I pointed to suggest we keep moving.

More relief on his part showed me I'd guessed right. Ethan wanted to take care of me. He wanted to make sure I had everything I needed. As far as he knew, I still needed him to support me like a pillar. And I did. But I also didn't.

My needs had evolved from a little girl who hero worshiped her big brother like a father. I'd done too much in his absence. Life had taught me lessons I couldn't ignore. He couldn't kiss the boo-boos to make them hurt less because I knew things didn't really work that way.

Later, I'd make sure he knew I still needed him. For now, he needed to see me doing okay with other people helping instead.

Was I doing okay?

Maybe.

CHAPTER 16

Mendez stayed behind with me while the guys handled another two alien encounters. They'd looted weapons from the first aliens, making their attacks swifter and more effective. For my benefit, they shoved bodies behind doors without letting me see them.

We reached the wormhole room without serious opposition. The aliens hadn't figured out we wanted to use it, or they didn't have enough personnel to post a guard outside it. Baldwin and Ethan breached the door. They called it clear without the sounds of a fight.

The moment I walked in, I knew the wormhole device had a problem. As before, white lights glowed from everywhere and nowhere. A giant gun-shaped thing with tubes and servos hung from an arm attached to the ceiling. Across the room from it, a round piece of metal bigger than Ethan stood on a platform with a ramp to the floor. Behind both, a glass wall separated the device from its bank of screen controls. Robots and empty docking stations lined the walls.

The gun-shaped part, which actually created the wormhole, pointed at the floor. The screens flickered from green to blue and back without a rhythm. Instead of reflecting light, the mirror had a flat gray surface.

Nothing about this device had the look of a functioning piece of equipment.

Baldwin closed the door once Mendez and I stepped inside and blocked it with his body. "Fire it up."

"I'll try. It looks messed up." Knowing the guys all wanted to get home as soon as possible, I hurried to the controls. Last time, I'd gotten lucky. The guys had accidentally activated the thing to pull me through. When we'd returned, it still had stood primed and ready to work. My efforts had reversed the beam and nothing more.

"Messed up?" Ethan walked around the gun-shaped part. "I guess I remember this pointing at the mirror." He gestured to the round piece of metal.

"Hey, that mirror ain't a mirror," Nash said.

Before we'd activated it the last time, the piece of metal had looked like a mirror, reflecting the room's contents.

I reached the screens and tapped one. Nothing happened. They kept flickering. Unwilling to give up this fast, I tapped every single screen. Then I flipped toggle switches. Since I'm not stupid, I did one at a time, then returned it to the previous position.

Halfway through this process, Ethan joined me behind the protective glass and leaned against the wall.

"What do you think is wrong with it?"

He wanted my best guess. I could give him that. "The power was knocked offline while it had a wormhole open. Like a power outage at home. When that happens to computers or other electronics, sometimes it screws them up. They need a diagnostic, then repair. Or it might've taken a power surge when the engines came back online. Something inside it could be fried."

"So this is a waste of time."

"Probably." Below the bottom row of screens and controls, I noticed a small plastic square like the strange one in my bag.

"Then we need a Plan C."

Crouching, I poked the square. It wiggled. "That first alien's ship is still here. I used it to send the signal to Akata. I don't know how to make it fly, but maybe we can use it for a diversion or something."

If that first square existed not attached to anything, maybe this one could too. I pulled. The square popped off the console. Looking it over, I didn't see a port of any kind, though I did find another circular symbol stamped on it. Where it had been, the console had a small indentation the size of the square with the same symbol in it.

Straightening, I tucked it into my bag as something to investigate later with Akata's help. In case that had caused some change, I tapped a few screens. Nothing.

"I'm not really sure what to make of you, Cog."

"You're not the same person either." I stepped beside him and slipped my arm around his back. Baldwin and Nash stood vigilant at the door. Mendez rapped the mirror with a knuckle.

Ethan draped his arm over my shoulders. "No, I guess I'm not." He sighed. We stood for a moment with me thinking we should get moving already. But Ethan stayed there, so I did too. "You like Mendez?"

"Sure." I shrugged. He'd seen Mendez helping me, so of course he'd ask about that. "I like all three of the guys. They're tons better people than my friends."

"No, I mean like wanting to date him."

I blinked like a moron. The thought hadn't even crossed my mind. Why would it? Between fleeing aliens, wriggling through the floor, trying to not barf, worrying about food, and getting Akata captured, I hadn't had time to think about that kind of stuff.

My gaze naturally drifted to him. Mendez had stopped knocking on the mirror. He walked around the platform, nudging the structure with his boot. His Latinx heritage gave him dark hair and eyes, and darker skin than Ethan and me. Otherwise, he and Ethan had been stamped from the same mold.

Aside from one black couple, all my friends back home

were white. I'd never spent much time around other kinds of people. Ethan hadn't either. At least, not until he'd joined the Marines.

Not that it mattered. These men, even the angry version of Baldwin, all had a horrifyingly huge amount of humanity and decency compared to my friends. They cared and wanted to help me. Like no one, ever, except Ethan.

But did I want to date Mendez?

What did that even mean out here? We couldn't go to movies or coffee shops. The next corner didn't have a bowling alley or a dance club. He couldn't buy me anything. Akata could give us privacy, I supposed, but I didn't really want that. Not now. Maybe later, but not now.

Come to think of it, I liked not having to hang on a guy's every word. Not acting like an accessory some jock flashed for status took so much less attention and effort. These guys treated me like I had value myself. As a person who knew things they didn't and could do things they couldn't.

Compared to all the guys I'd ever dated, these Marines were aliens.

Between Nash, Baldwin, and Mendez, I didn't know if I'd pick Mendez. Baldwin had a little more of a temper than I liked, but I thought he'd treat me well if he could transition to civilian life without exploding. Nash didn't seem like he had any downsides. Neither did Mendez.

Mendez noticed me watching him. He smiled, then he turned his attention back to the platform as if he considered disassembling it.

I blushed because now I knew he had feelings for me. Boyfriends didn't want to listen to their girls talk, though. Why did he offer that?

Ethan nudged my shoulder, shaking my thoughts loose. "Still with us?"

Nodding, I blushed harder. "I don't know. About Mendez, I mean. Did he ask you to ask me?"

He snorted. "No. We're not fourteen."

All my friends acted like that still at seventeen and eighteen, so I didn't know what he meant. "Then why did you ask?"

"While we sat in that cell like lumps, it was pointed out to me that I've been acting like an overprotective dad worried about his baby girl princess's virtue. Also that you're eighteen and a high school graduate, which makes you an adult." He squeezed my shoulders. "I realized I've been acting like that because we haven't traded letters for two years, which means you're frozen for me at sixteen. And because I noticed Mendez looking at you, saying things, and doing things. He's acting like a suitor chasing an easily startled rabbit."

The idea of Mendez wearing a tuxedo and stalking a bunny with an engagement ring on a carrot popped into my head. I covered my mouth and giggled.

"If you want him to back off, I can take care of that for you. If you don't…" He made a series of faces like he had to chew a lemon. "I can keep my mouth shut and let it happen or not."

Mendez jogged to the glass wall and leaned around it. "Hey boss, are we taking the fast track ride home or not?" He looked at Ethan.

I answered. "No. I think it needs rebooting, and I have no idea how to manage that."

Ethan pushed me off the wall with a gentle nudge. "We should find Akata, free her, and get off this hellhole. Ten bucks says the aliens will fix the wormhole thing for us. Then we can come back and use it when they least expect it." He reached for my hand, then changed his mind and waved for both of us to follow.

How did I act with Mendez now that I knew what he wanted from me? Except I didn't know. He didn't act like any other guy who'd ever wanted to date me. Mendez didn't pat my ass or size me up. So far, other than a hug I'd desperately needed and some protective shielding, he'd barely touched me. A kiss on the head and another on the forehead reminded me more of Ethan than a boyfriend.

He'd promised to listen to me. No boyfriend did that.

Hoping I didn't seem awkward, I flashed Mendez a smile and hurried to follow Ethan.

CHAPTER 17

Baldwin opened the door and peered in both directions. He closed the door again. "There's a pair headed this way. They might walk past."

"We'll take them down if they come inside." Ethan gestured for Mendez and me to hide against the wall.

I hesitated, then blurted out the thing I wanted to say. "Could you not kill them?"

"There's no time for this," Mendez said.

Did lots of people have to die for us to escape? I didn't think so. But I needed a reason. Like, for example, the expertise required to repair the machine behind me. "We need them to fix the wormhole device. They might have to bring in more aliens to fix it if we kill too many, which would just make returning harder."

Ethan frowned at the floor.

Nash shrugged. "She's got a point. And these weapons don't kill, they stun. Killing actually takes more time."

"Dead men can't talk," Baldwin said.

Mendez glanced at me. "We can make an effort to hit them before they see us."

"We strive for zero kills from here on out," Ethan said. "But also zero recognition."

The doors opened, giving me no chance to argue with the order. Ethan and Baldwin fired their stolen alien tasers.

Both intruders jerked with the shock and collapsed.

Ethan and Nash dragged the two unconscious aliens into the room by their feet. Baldwin kept watch. Mendez stuck with me.

"Cog, best guess where we'll find Akata?"

If the aliens wanted to try boarding her, they'd need an airlock. Since they'd hauled her from the prisoner docking ring, I didn't think they'd return her there. "The docking corridor with the other ships."

"Mendez, go scout the stairwell and corridor down there," Ethan said.

I blinked. So far, they'd done everything as a group. "By himself?" My belly tightened at the idea of Mendez creeping around the station on his own. Tons of things could go wrong, and no one would know.

Mendez, unconcerned, hustled out of the room. Baldwin closed the doors.

"Yes," Ethan said, "by himself. We'd ordinarily do that in pairs, but he shouldn't have a problem for such a short run."

Did Mendez have to do this? Why not Baldwin? Ethan always put Baldwin on point. "What if aliens shoot him?"

"I'll hear it on our comms."

They had comms. All this time, they'd retained the ability to talk to each other over radios, and I hadn't realized it. Next time, I'd have one. This whole episode would've worked much differently if I could've talked to Ethan all along. He would've reminded me about the weapons, which would've kept Akata safe.

Nash patted my shoulder. "He'll be fine."

These guys trusted me to know my stuff and asked me to trust them to know their stuff in return. I rubbed my face. My body felt heavy and dumb. How much sleep had I gotten? Not enough.

"Eat," Nash said. "It helps keep you going when you're tired."

My lip curled and I knew it. Food didn't solve

problems, it created them. "I'm not hungry."

Because life hates me, my stomach growled.

Nash raised his brow.

I grumbled without words as I sat and pulled off my backpack. "I wasn't until you said something."

He snickered.

Jerk. The bar I shoved into my face tasted as blah as the others. I didn't want any of those, and I didn't want this one. By the time I finished it, though, my stomach had stopped gurgling.

Someone knocked on the door three times. Baldwin let Mendez back into the room.

Mendez took a moment to breathe as he stepped up to report to Ethan. "They've got the corridor covered. Two pairs patrolling, another pair at three different airlocks, plus another four spaced along it."

Ethan furrowed his brow. "If we go in guns blazing, they'll have too many chances to hit us. That corridor doesn't have anywhere to hide."

"It kind of does?" I hadn't explained my method of transit across the station and back, so I told them how I'd reached the docking corridor and escaped the residence area.

All four men stared at me. For a long time.

"Chica." Mendez sprouted a wide grin. "You've got some serious *cojones*."

Ethan smacked his arm. "Could the rest of us get through that way?"

"No, the space is too narrow." I frowned and tried to think of a way me getting back to either spot would help anything. "I could go back to the dorm room and open up the panel above it. That'd be the floor on this level. I don't know where it is, but once I come through, I can figure out my way and bring you guys there."

Mendez had said they guarded three airlocks. I turned to him. "Two guarded airlocks are left of the door but not too far down, right? Where's the third?"

"Way at the end on the left."

"That'll be Akata. I could open up those panels instead. If I can find them. Then you could all drop down in front of Akata's airlock instead of trying to sneak there."

"Good plan," Baldwin said.

"Agreed." Ethan nodded. "We should be able to figure out approximately where it is from up here, though."

"Getting into the dorm room might still do us some good," Nash said. "We could split up and cause a diversion. That'd make getting to Akata's airlock easier for half the team."

"And the other half?" Mendez asked.

"The airlock you usually use?" I suggested. "Would they guard that? It didn't seem like the rest of the access points."

Ethan reached toward me like he meant to tousle my hair. He paused and patted me on the shoulder instead. "Okay. Two simultaneous missions. One team scouts Akata's usual access point. The other team goes hunting for the panel section above her airlock."

This plan sounded great. Except for one tiny detail. "Before we do anything serious, we have to confirm Akata is conscious. How do we do that?"

The guys glanced at each other.

I cleared my throat in the silence. "Maybe we should also figure out how to disable the weapons?"

"See?" Mendez said, beaming at me. "Everybody needs a team."

"And every team needs an engineer," Ethan said. "Let's work on the weapons first. What do we know about them?"

"The sentinels are mounted on the struts for the spinning rings," Mendez said. "They fire a concussive blast that affects living things more than non-living things. They don't usually target Akata, which we think is because of her size."

"That's it," Nash said with a nod.

The station had four spinning rings to produce gravity

for the station. Mounting them on those rings meant they had to use computers for targeting. No organic brain could calculate trajectories that complex fast enough to hit anything.

Why not mount them on something stationary, like sensible people?

The same reason they didn't use rivets, probably.

"If I can figure out how to shut down power to those rings, that would kill gravity and also stop the weapons. We'd have to kill the power to all the rings at once, though. One by one would give them too much warning. And I don't know how to do it."

We stood in a circle, everyone frowning at the floor in thought. I noticed they'd positioned themselves to consider me equal. No one else had ever done that.

"If you shut off the engines," Ethan asked, "can we get the airlocks to work?"

"The one Akata usually uses would work," Mendez said. "Can't speak for the other."

Nash pointed at me. "You sent a message to Akata before. You could do it again. Tell her to get on over to our usual breach point. Tell her we're taking the station offline so they can't shoot her."

"Wait." I held up a hand and had to think something through, because the whole sentinels thing didn't make sense. Pinpointing why took me a minute. "If the sentinels have never targeted her before, and they only started targeting her the first time after the alien showed up, doesn't that mean someone would have to manually select her as a target for them to hit her?"

"Yes," Baldwin said. "Take them down, Akata's safe."

"Where are they?' Ethan asked.

"Not in the residence area," I said. "Not in the docking corridor either. Not in this room, and not in the prisoner cells. No one would put that in any medical bay. The controls would all go together in case they ever need to get extra tools or supplies from one to another. I get the feeling most of this station isn't fully accessible or intended for people. It has a lot of automation. The engines are huge. The wormhole generator is probably much more complex and huge than it looks."

"Where would you put it?" Mendez asked.

I would've created a master control room in the center of the station and made it the most secure piece of the whole facility. Around that, I would've put the residence area so all the workers could provide an extra layer of passive defense. But I did things logically with humans in mind. These aliens did not. At least, not according to any design principles I'd learned.

"I think the engines are in the middle. I didn't go up high enough to see if that was true, and it's total darkness in that crawlspace. It could've been right over my head the whole time, and I never would've known. This room is near one end of the station, and your usual access point is at the other end. This level has the prison cells, which makes sense because abductees get herded there from the wormhole room. The residence and docking corridor are on the level below.

"Since they put the screens room in the residence, I think it's plausible they also put weapons control in a residence area. But," I held up a finger. "I think there's more than one residence area, and we haven't found the others."

"There could be ten access points from that docking corridor and we wouldn't know it," Ethan said. "All we've ever done through there is run, so if doors are closed, or light is low, we wouldn't have noticed them."

I nodded because I wouldn't have noticed them either. "Most likely, weapons control will be at the midpoint. Because they use wires to connect everything, and that would keep the wire lengths equal, which is better for manufacturing. In theory. They wouldn't bother for the screens room since there are a zillion cameras all over the place."

The idea of laying that much black wire goo boggled my mind. Creating the full design for this station must've taken a lot of effort. Then again, designing and building a skyscraper took that much effort too, and people did that all the time. People had done that before computers, even. Just not in space.

"So where's the midpoint?" Mendez asked.

"No idea," I said.

CHAPTER 18

If I wanted to wriggle through the floors for a while, I could find the midpoint. Did I have the energy for that? Maybe? "But if you can hole up someplace, I can look for it."

"We need a room with one chokepoint entrance, an emergency exit, and a low likelihood they'll look for us there." Ethan pointed at me. "Let's find that dorm room first. We can sit there and take down anyone who comes looking while we wait. Akata gets time to recuperate."

Emma didn't get time to recuperate, but I'd live. I nodded. "I don't suppose we have a flashlight?"

"Sorry, chica. But here's a taser." Mendez offered me his alien weapon. "You might need it."

I stared at it.

"It won't kill nobody," Nash said.

I'd taken two hits from one of these things. "It hurts, though."

"Cog." Ethan took the taser from Mendez's hand and stuck it in mine. "If you don't tag them first, they'll be happy to zap you. That's how this works. We killed those aliens because they want to take us prisoner and make us do what they want. These people are slavemasters.

"I don't expect you to punch anyone in the face, or to sneak like a ninja. I don't want you to have to zap someone with this thing. But if you find yourself face to face with these aliens, I want you to remember that you matter to me."

"You matter to me too, chica."

Baldwin grunted. Nash murmured his assent.

"Also," Ethan added with half a grin, "we can't get home without you."

My eyes burned. I needed to sleep because then I wouldn't want to cry about anything for a while.

Taking the taser, I nodded. "It's that way compared to the prison cells, and almost all the way to the side wall."

"Baldwin, take point," Ethan said. "We're escorting Emma back to the cells."

Mendez patted his ear. "Boss, maybe one of us should give up our radio to her. If she's going to crawl around in the station guts, being able to talk to us might help."

"She can use mine." Baldwin popped out his earbud and removed his mic. A thin wire connected both pieces to a handheld unit like a walkie-talkie that he carried in his pocket.

Ethan helped me strap it to myself after I wiped off the earbud. I liked Baldwin and all, but I didn't need his earwax. The earbud felt the same as any other earbud. We swapped some stuff out of my bag and put the control unit into it. This time, I wouldn't have to carry around two backpacks.

Not that I'd needed more than the extra canteen. Live and learn, right?

We jogged back to the prison cells and found no aliens along the way. Small favors. Either they hadn't noticed the guys missing from their cell yet or they'd noticed, checked the cell, and moved on to searching while we'd stayed in the wormhole room.

These aliens so far hadn't seemed particularly observant. Maybe they'd turned to abducting other races for a lot of reasons. Another idea wriggled in the back of my mind, about the tech and why they built such clunky robots, but I couldn't put my finger on it.

Ethan helped me settle into the floor again. Mendez

handed me the scissors and putty knife I'd need to cut the panel sealant. Baldwin and Nash started ripping out the other wall panels, looking for other cameras.

"The mics are push-to-talk," Ethan said. He pushed my finger against the button at my neck. We'd already done a mic check, so we knew it worked. He let go.

I tested the amount of effort I needed to make it work. A tiny prod on the side of my neck handled it. Good.

Once I'd finished testing it, Ethan continued. "Check in when you reach the midpoint. That'll give us something to go on for how far it is. Check in again when you hit the dorm room, then when you've got the upper panel open. Don't worry about opening it all the way, just get it started. We'll pull it off from above."

I looked ahead, into darkness. Not having to do all the things sounded good to me. "This teamwork thing seems a lot less exhausting."

"That's how it works, chica. As you move, keep your pace steady. That'll help us gauge the distance." Mendez held up a fist. "See you on the other side."

Why did he—? Oh. Duh. I bumped his fist. Then I pushed myself into the darkness.

I could do this. My arms ached. My legs ached. My core ached. That knock to the skull earlier had faded, letting me experience the full weight of my weariness. At least I didn't have the energy to let my mind wander.

Sometime between forever and a half, I reached the wide gap of the central support. "Checking in at the midpoint."

"Girl can move," Nash said into my ear.

"Girl can also hear you," I said.

Mendez laughed into his open mic.

"Less chatter," Ethan said.

"Yes sir, Sergeant sir."

"You don't call a Sergeant 'sir,' chica. He works for a living."

"We're all working for a living. Hang on. D'ya think they'll give us back pay when we get home?" Nash asked.

"This is the opposite of cutting the chatter."

I giggled at Ethan without sending it through the mic.

The guys stopped talking, so I did too. Knowing I could push a button and hear them made the work less tedious, though. I felt less alone and desperate than I had the first time through the darkness.

Next time, I wanted to bring a flashlight and something more useful for cutting than a putty knife. Knife through butter, it did not do. Most of the reason I needed rest boiled down to shoving a small blade through a rubbery, uncooperative substance. The rest probably had a lot to do with not sleeping.

Before I shifted sideways to find the dorm room, I noted the tiny star of light from the docking corridor in the distance. Both it and the prison cell seemed so far away. I'd covered huge distances crossing the station back and forth.

Ducking through the holes in the supports, I tried to keep my speed even. My knee slipped once, giving me a heart attack. I didn't fall. I thought I had for a moment, then that moment passed. Pure determination kept me going when I wanted to curl into a ball and sleep.

When I found the light for the dorm room, it looked like a shorter trek than the docking corridor. Thank goodness for that. I needed to stop. Though I wanted to get there as fast as possible, I forced myself to keep to the same pace.

"Leaving the midpoint passage to move laterally again."

"'Laterally' is a big word," Nash said.

Did he mean that, or was he teasing? "I don't think you're likely to have a solid understanding of what's big or not."

For a moment, I thought I'd offended all the guys. They didn't respond at all.

"Shame you didn't grab antiseptic in the med bay,

chica," Mendez said. I could tell he wore a grin about five miles wide. "I think Nash might need it after that burn."

Relief I hadn't crossed some line made me laugh. I had to cover my mouth to keep it quiet.

"Shut it," Ethan snapped, harsh and curt.

All my amusement evaporated in an instant. Had I upset him? Did something bad happen? I kept moving because I'd promised too, but I also waited to hear some kind of resolution.

"Harper is hit," a voice grunted, low, quiet, and unidentifiable.

I sucked in a breath and didn't know what to do.

"Target down."

"Eyes on target."

"Target down."

"Two left."

They all used that same strange, low-volume speech, so I couldn't tell which voice belonged to which guy. I wanted to do something.

Like what? Pop out of the floor and zap somebody? As if I could. The panel would take too long to saw through, and I'd never find the right one in time.

"Nash is hit."

"No, I'm good. Near miss."

Right. Baldwin didn't have a radio, so with Ethan down, I only had two voices to track. Nash had that light Southern drawl, even in a whisper.

"Is Ethan okay?" I had to know.

"He got zapped, chica. Baldwin is covering him. He'll be fine when it wears off. Keep moving and get that floor cut open."

Okay. I could do that. I kept moving toward the light. Maybe I sped up more than I should have, but I didn't care. The sooner we got Ethan someplace safe, the better off everyone would be.

"I'm at the dorm room." As quietly as I could, I

checked inside the room. Still empty, and no sign of anyone having come and gone. "It's clear. I'm starting on the panel above." So I had a solid base to lie on, I attacked the next panel over, not the one directly above my loosened one.

"We're fine, chica. Targets are down. We're all good. Bang the scissors on the floor once right now."

I stopped cutting to whack the panel above me with the scissors. "Did you hear that?"

"No, but we're still on the move."

What if I broke into a room full of aliens? What if they heard me and stood around the panel with tasers, waiting to zap the rat in their walls? I gulped and asked the question I needed to ask. "Should I do it again?"

"No. Not until I ask so we know to listen for it."

Thank goodness. Determined to get through the panel, no matter what I faced on the other side, I got back to work.

CHAPTER 19

The next time I whacked on the panel, Mendez still didn't hear it. I kept working. When I had one edge cut free, we tried again.

"I think I heard that," Nash said. "One more, Emma."

I smacked that panel with the scissors as hard as I could.

"Yep. I heard it."

"Chica, do a bunch of small hits. Tap the panel."

Still holding the scissors by the blades, I tapped the panel several times. "I can't do that and cut around the corner at the same time."

"It's okay. Deep breath, chica. We're not in a hurry. Keep tapping."

Tap, tap, tap. This felt stupid. Instead of cutting, instead of getting something done, I had to make noise. Without something more concrete to focus on, I imagined a pair of aliens prepping their tasers for both me and the guys.

"We may have a problem," Mendez murmured into my ear.

I froze. "What kind?"

"There's a robot. It's active, and it's sitting near where we think you might be."

If I kept cutting through, and the robot sat on top of the panel over me, would it crush me?

No, of course not, Emma. Stop thinking stupid. The support beams protected me. So long as I had the panel between us, I had nothing to worry about. In a relative sense. A robot didn't sound better than aliens, except that I knew its programming couldn't handle clever.

I probably couldn't handle clever at the moment either, but never mind that.

"I don't think it's on your panel, at least. Keep cutting if you can, chica. We're going to distract it."

Distract it? "Are you crazy?"

"Naw, we're Marines."

Which meant yes.

Cutting. I would think about cutting the sealant. Nothing else mattered except getting through the stupid panel so we could get Ethan into the dorm room. He would recover, we'd move on to the next stage of the plan, and Akata would wake up in time to rescue us all. Absolutely nothing could possibly go wrong.

Except for everything, of course.

I jammed the putty knife into the sealant past the corner and worked on opening the second side.

"I'm fine, Cog." Ethan sounded like crap with a side of crap and some crap gravy on top. "You're doing great. Keep working."

I swallowed a lump in my throat. "Fine is what you say when you don't want to talk about it."

Ethan chuckled. "I'm okay, Cog. No actual injuries, just waiting for my brain to settle after getting scrambled by a blender. Mendez and Nash are leading the robot away. Baldwin is watching over me. I want you to tap on the panel again so Baldwin can find it. Tap, tap, tap."

"I can do that." Leaving the scalpel stuck in the sealant, I clunked the scissors handle against the panel above me, over and over.

"That's perfect, Cog. Keep doing it."

After half a minute of tapping, Ethan said, "Can you

hear Baldwin? He's standing right over you."

"No. But I can push up." I stowed the scissors, then braced my arm and hand against the floor. Pushing upward with my shoulder, I thought I managed to bow the panel a tiny bit.

"So here's the thing, Cog. The panel you picked is in the middle of a hallway."

Of course it was. I relaxed. "I can't do the next one. It's over the hole. I won't have any leverage. If I do the one on the other side, you guys won't fit through."

"Good to know." He went quiet for several seconds. "Push up against the loose corner as much as you can and see if you can pass the scissors or knife to Baldwin."

I put my feet into it and shoved the scissors through the gap. They left my hand before I got them all the way. After that, I pushed through the putty knife. Baldwin took that before I let go too.

"Good work, Cog. Now get into the room, relax, and let us take it from here."

Having a team really helped a lot. I slid down into the room and let myself lay on the bed not under the open panel.

"We lost the robot," Mendez said. "No new hostiles. Returning to your position, Sergeant."

Sometimes they sounded so serious and regimental. Other times, they cracked jokes. I didn't quite understand where they drew the line.

"Good work," Ethan said.

I closed my eyes.

Half a minute later, Ethan shook me. "Hey. You fell asleep."

Sitting up, I wrapped my arms around his neck and squeezed. "I didn't mean to."

Nash sat at the front door, bracing it shut with his body. Mendez and Baldwin sat on the other bed. I'd slept through them ripping down the panel and setting it aside. Light didn't shine through the ceiling, though.

"Always nap when you can, chica," Mendez said. He pushed a paper-wrapped bar at my face.

Baldwin grunted his assent.

I took the bar and let go of Ethan. As I stuffed the food in my mouth, I pointed at the ceiling and made a questioning noise.

"We left the panel above sitting there," Ethan said "So long as no one takes a close look, they won't notice it's loose. Do you feel up to taking on the next part of this plan? Because it's on you again. We need you to find us an access to the area with weapons control."

Frowning at my bar, I tried to see a map of the station in my head. "I wish I knew which direction to go from here."

"That stairwell we keep using isn't in the middle," Mendez said. "The docking corridor stretches in both directions. If I had to put on money on it, I'd say it's not at the center. I think you need to go toward the docking doors they're using. Which is…" He closed his eyes and held up both fingers, trying to orient.

"That way." I pointed because I'd been in and out of this whole area enough to know by now. This room connected to a hallway perpendicular to the docking corridor. "I don't know how far. Or how to gauge how far I'm going in the dark."

Baldwin looked up. "Count beams."

I looked up too. How had I not even thought of that? "I'm tired," I whined.

Ethan patted my knee. "I could tell by how you passed out cold. We'll take some time to rest up after we free Akata and get off this hellhole."

Nodding, I finished the rest of my bar. Mendez passed me a canteen, and I took a few sips. "How many beams should I count?"

No one had an answer for that, which made me feel less dumb.

If the small ship's docking door hit near the center, and I could find that tunnel, then I could count beams to there. Or maybe I didn't need to. "There's about two feet of space between them," I said, thinking out loud. "The basic panels are four feet wide, so technically, each has two beams of its own. This room has two basic panels across and three in length. That makes it eight feet by twelve feet.

"So far, aside from wall sections with doors, I haven't seen any partial panels. They tend to use four feet as their basic unit of measure. Can someone check how many panels across the hallway outside is?"

Nash hopped to his feet and cracked the door open. He peered through the crack, then held up a hand with three fingers.

I knew I needed to get some serious sleep because this simple math took effort.

"That's six total to reach the other side of the hall." I closed my eyes and pictured the layout from my first visit to this section. I'd peeked inside all the rooms. "This section had more dorm rooms on the other side of the hall, and a communal bathroom. That means it's another three panels across. Accounting for three walls between here and there, the next set of living quarters should be about forty feet over from this edge, which is twenty beams. Maybe nineteen, because the walls aren't that thick."

"Harper," Mendez said, "have I mentioned lately that your sister is really smart?"

I grinned at him.

Ethan rolled his eyes. "Go find us the weapons controls, Cog."

"Yes, Sergeant." I stood and waved for Baldwin and Mendez to move. "I need a boost, please."

Mendez got a twinkle in his eyes like he thought he could take advantage of the opportunity. At least, that's what any other guy would do.

Baldwin stood on the bed. Mendez knelt beside me and made a cup with his hands. I stuck my boot in Mendez's hands, Baldwin steadied me with his hands on my hips, and they lifted me into the crawlspace without touching anything more risqué than the outside of my thigh. And Baldwin only did that because I leaned a little too far to the side.

These guys made me want to cry for being such intense gentlemen. Mendez had to know Ethan had told me about his interest, and he still didn't do anything. Any other guy would've proceeded to help in this situation by at least shoving against my ass, if not feeling me up.

"I'm taking out my earbud to grab a nap," Ethan said. "If you need anything, Nash and Mendez are on watch."

Oh good. That meant Mendez could say anything without Ethan hearing it. Nash would hear it, but I doubted he'd ever say a word unless Mendez said something awful.

I wriggled to the midpoint, half-expecting Mendez to start talking dirty into my ear. He didn't. Neither he nor Nash spoke. Along the way, I counted panel boundaries to the center.

"Checking in at the midline. Fifty panels to here."

"So that's how far?" Mendez asked.

"Two hundred feet, plus a bit to account for walls. Maybe an extra twenty feet. I wasn't counting that part." I wedged my body into the center line. "I'd guess the station is approximately six hundred feet wide, excluding the outer hull. So maybe a total of seven hundred feet. Or, for a Marine, that'd be about two football fields including the end zones."

Both men chuckled.

"That's pretty darn big," Nash said. "And it's a heckuva lot bigger the long way. You got a guess for that?"

"Based upon the rendering I've seen, the dimensional ratio is pretty high. It's got to be at least, oh, four or five thousand feet long. That's between about thirteen and sixteen football fields. But now I have to count beams, so I can't be your calculator anymore."

"Day-umn. This station is huge."

"I think we already knew that," I said.

Then I started counting.

CHAPTER 20

One, two, slip through a cross brace, three, four, slip through a cross brace. If I counted ten cross braces, I'd probably hit close enough.

"Emma?"

"Yeah?" Three cross braces.

"Why does Harper call you 'Cog'?" When I didn't answer right away, Mendez added, "It can wait. Counting is more important."

Four. I paused and tried to decide how to word my answer. "I think it probably says more about him than me, so maybe that's his story to tell. Short version is I've always liked gears and machines, and he noticed."

"Would you mind if someone else called you that?"

Five. "It would be weird? So yes?"

"Okay. No problem. Just wondering."

Sure, Mendez, just wondering. No reason. Six. Seven.

"Why is it he has a nickname for you, but you don't have one for him?"

Eight and I stopped, because no one had ever asked me that before. Mom and Dad had overheard Ethan calling me Cog, and they'd asked if it bothered me or made me feel weird. Some of my friends had gotten into my stash of his letters and noticed he used that name to address me. They'd teased me about it.

The fact he'd signed the letters with his name had never given anyone pause.

"I had a hard time with the 'th' sound when I was little, so it took me forever to say his name right." Nine. "Until somewhere between six and seven, the best I could manage was either Efan or Etan. So it was a pretty big deal when I could finally say it right and do it consistently."

Ten. I stopped and noticed the light at the end. Given the level, I'd found my access for the docking corridor. If I'd only known, right?

"I'll bet that was adorable, you running around calling him Efan with your red curls."

While I didn't want to tell Mendez to shut up, I needed him to shut up. "I have to count panels now. If you interrupt me and I lose count, I'll have to come back to where I am now and start over."

"Understood, Emma. Tell us when you reach the spot. Radio silence until then."

And just like that, Mendez shut up. I waited half a minute to make sure he didn't wheedle. Nothing. How did I manage to wind up in a different galaxy with a group of guys so incredibly good, kind, and decent as these? And they were all Marines. Didn't military men swear every other word and drink and hire hookers?

Never mind. I needed to count. With the assurance Mendez and Nash wouldn't say anything outside of an emergency, I wriggled into the space and counted panels as I passed the seams. At fifty, I stopped, found the edge I thought I needed, and started cutting.

"I'm at the panel. It'd be nice if one of you could talk to me while I saw at this sealant stuff. It's kind of hard and boring."

Mendez huffed a laugh. "That sounds like the worst night ever."

I rolled my eyes. "Let's not talk about that, though. Tell me…I dunno. Tell me why you joined the Marines."

"Better than the Chair Force," Mendez said.

"And the Navy is full of—" Nash coughed. "Ah, I mean, my family has a long history of service in the Marines."

Uh-huh. Neither had answered the question, so I dropped it. Maybe they considered it too personal.

"Do either of you have a girl back home?" I hoped I sounded casual.

"I did," Nash said, "but I imagine she's moved on by now, presuming me dead. Which is fair. It'll probably be pretty awkward for her when I get home. I'm really more eager to see my family anyway. My Momma is a great cook." He rambled for a while about all the things his mother made better than anyone else in the universe.

I'd never heard of half the dishes he mentioned, but the sound of his voice kept me going. When I finished cutting out a corner, I checked the room. No one was inside it, and no weapons pointed at my face. Thanks to math, I'd actually found another dorm room, so I didn't have to go searching elsewhere. The panel I'd cut even hung over the bed on the same side.

Nash trailed off, probably thinking about the gourmet feast he'd have when he returned home. I wanted, more than ever, to make sure he could have that.

"I'm through," I said. Notably, Mendez hadn't answered the question. I thought I might hear about it later. "Going to check for the weapons control room."

"Don't take risks you don't have to, chica. We can find the spot above and go through again."

I smiled as I cracked the door open. "Yeah, but then you have to wake up Baldwin. I bet he's cranky when you do that."

Mendez and Nash both laughed, then cut off their mics.

Seeing no one to the left, I opened the door and checked to the right. As expected, this residential area mimicked the other in a mirror image. They'd flipped it, probably to use the same plumbing for both bathrooms. Having a single, large bathroom would've made more sense, but I hadn't investigated it fully. Maybe they had a connecting section.

Not that the bathroom mattered.

Okay, it mattered a little. I'd had water and food, and a lot of time had passed. The prison cells didn't have bathroom facilities.

Anyway. I ran to the open door at the end, where the other area had the screens room. Peeking around the corner, I saw an alien sitting at a console in the back corner of the room. If I made a big movement, I thought he'd see me, either out of the corner of his eye or as a reflection in his screens.

The screens showed star fields, a nearby star, a nearby planet, and Akata. I checked behind me to make sure no one sneaked up while I wasn't paying attention, then I wrapped my hand around the taser in my bag.

If I zapped this guy and shut the door, no one would know. But he might wake up soon enough to stop us. I could zap him twice so he passed out, then drag him to a room and tie him up with…a bed sheet? A different room than the one I used, though. When he woke up, he wouldn't see the open panel.

All I had to do was shoot him. Leaning against the wall beside the door, I breathed. I could do this. One, two, three, then zap, and then zap again. Drag him out, shut the door, stash him, and let the guys know I took care of it.

In my head, it sounded easy. I remembered how those tasers felt, though. Doing that to someone else hurt a piece of me.

Except Ethan had said they'd treated the guys like slaves. Those backpacks suggested they cared whether their slaves lived or died, but not much more. Taking people from their homeworlds to fight a war they knew nothing about was evil. Since they kept doing it, that meant they got people killed.

Which meant they didn't care about those deaths. They thought of us as animals. On second thought, they thought of us as tools. When an animal gets hurt, you try to help it. When a tool gets broken, you throw it out.

The taser wouldn't kill this guy, it'd just make him hurt for a while. Then he'd recover. Aside from his pride, maybe.

I leaned around the corner, pointed the taser at the alien's back and pushed the button. Blue-white energy arced from the tip to the alien. His body jerked. Cringing at what I saw, I pushed the button again.

He slumped over the console.

My hand shook.

I ducked inside the room and shut the door. Breathe. In through the nose, out through the mouth. The alien's back rose and fell, proving he still breathed. The taser hadn't killed him, thank goodness.

"Target down. Weapons control room secured."

"Damn, chica, you sound like a Marine. How many times did you zap him? Did he see you?"

Did that count as a compliment or not? He probably meant it as one, so I took it that way. "Twice, and no. He's unconscious. Hit him in the back. I'm going to see if I can disable some of this equipment."

I shoved the alien aside. He fell into a boneless heap on the floor. Probably, that hadn't caused him any serious harm. If I wanted to, I could've done anything to him. He looked a lot like the alien who'd tased me.

If I could avoid it, I didn't want to get enough experience with these aliens to tell them apart.

"Don't take too long," Nash said. "The sooner we get outta here, the better."

Right. I took a closer look at the screen showing Akata. Their tractor beams had a visible component, so I knew they'd turned it off. Tapping the screen in the center got me a closer view, which seemed like a miracle. The thing did what I wanted, and it made sense!

They'd looped cables around her lumpy body as if that would stop her.

Then again, maybe it would, since she hadn't left. Unless they'd killed her after all.

No, I would not think that. Akata had been stunned, maybe knocked unconscious. If the sentinel bolts worked on her like the tasers worked on us, she had already awakened. She wouldn't leave without us. Did I need to send her a message?

"How would I know by looking if Akata is awake?"

"No idea, chica. We've never seen much of her outer shell."

I examined the image, hoping for some sign of life. She didn't expand and contract like the alien breathing on the floor. The ship hung in the cables, seemingly suspended by them. "Do I need to find a way to send her a message?"

"She'll see us when we open the airlock inside her protective field. That's how we've always done it. She doesn't usually sit there with the door open while we scout."

One problem solved, one still unknown.

I checked for a way to pull wires or plugs, or anything else that might make this console harder to use.

Wait. If the aliens noticed I'd done something here, nothing bad happened to me. We didn't need to leave no trace. They knew we'd escaped. Whatever damage I caused, they'd have to repair. I hefted my scissors. Making the weapons harder to use for a long term sounded good to me.

Aiming for the center of a screen with a star field, I stabbed with all the force I could muster. The scissor points smashed through the screen easier than I expected. My punctures caused the surface to spiderweb, and I whacked the handle against it to make the glass fall out.

Since I didn't want to waste too much time, I repeated that for each screen without specifically trying to cause more damage behind the glass. Replacing all the glass surfaces would cause them enough trouble. Without the screens, they had nothing to target.

Before leaving, I did notice another of those curious small squares in another of those curious indentations. This third one joined the other two in my bag. I had a feeling they acted as security keys, or maybe stored data. Akata could analyze them later.

"Weapons control disabled enough, I think. I'm going to zap this guy again and hide him in a different room."

"You go, girl," Nash said. "Let us know when you hit the centerline, and we'll wake up Harper and Baldwin."

I checked outside the door, then dragged my hostage to a different dorm room. After I tied him up, I zapped him again and left.

This time, I didn't bonk my head while jumping into the ceiling. Go me.

CHAPTER 21

At the centerline, I checked in as requested. By the time I returned, Ethan and Baldwin sat up and seemed alert enough not to do anything stupid.

Mendez helped me climb down without falling. Once again, he didn't touch me any more than he needed to, and his hands didn't stray anywhere questionable. He seemed content to help and do nothing more.

Ethan tucked in his earbud as I settled beside him on the edge of the bed. "I'm not going to pick who does what this time. Two of us need to run a diversion, and the other two need to go with Emma. Both missions have high risk. Whoever goes with Emma gets off the station faster, but has to deal with the possibility the aliens have some other way to control the weapons. And also that the diversion won't work on everyone. The diversion team has to create a diversion, and we all know how that works."

He shifted his gaze between the three men. "Obviously, I'd like to go with Emma. I won't if two of you have a strong need to go deal with that instead."

"I need my mic back if I don't go with Emma," Baldwin said. "Can't do distraction without connection."

Hearing that as a request, I pulled the walkie-talkie part out of my bag and handed it to him. He helped me remove the rest of it.

"Distraction," Mendez said.

How did I feel about that? Queasy, confused, uncertain. Did he say that to impress me? To see if I'd beg him to come with me? Some other reason that had nothing to do with me? Now that I knew he had interest, I didn't understand his behavior. Before, he'd seemed polite, friendly, and welcoming. Now…I had no idea.

Mendez didn't look at me, which made everything more confusing. He checked his weapon and retied a shoelace, every movement casual. Like he'd volunteered to go fetch pizza instead of purposely attract attention from hostile aliens.

"I don't rightly know which I'd be better for," Nash said. "That being the case, I'll take distraction so you can go with Emma."

"I'm rested," Baldwin said as he strapped on his mic. "You go to Akata."

"That's fair," Nash said.

Ethan nodded. He stood. Everyone else followed his lead. "Report as often as you can. Let us know when you reach the airlock. We'll wait five minutes after you start your distraction. Don't get shot or caught."

"Yes, Sergeant," both men intoned.

Mendez kissed my cheek and hopped onto the bed. He gripped the exposed support beam and lifted himself with so little effort I couldn't help but stare. At the top, he did magic to stay up there and also push the loose panel aside. He checked in every direction.

"Clear." Then he climbed up, just like that.

Baldwin followed him. They replaced the loose panel.

"Close your mouth, Cog." Ethan pushed my jaw closed with two fingers. "We can all do that. You could too if you ate right and practiced pull-ups every day."

I smacked his side with the back of my hand. "I've eaten more today than I did for the whole week before graduation." With a start, I realized the truth of that. Sure, I'd had some thoughts about purging, and I'd tried to resist the food, but I'd eaten it all and digested it. Once the food had gone down the hatch, I hadn't had time to think about what it did inside me.

And how did I feel? Tired. Used up and spit out. I needed to sleep. Once we reached Akata, I hoped they would let me go to bed while he picked up Mendez and Baldwin. On second thought, I wanted to know they'd reached Akata safely. I'd sit up and wait.

Ethan pulled me into a hug and kissed the top of my head. "Good. Let's continue that trend."

"Did Mendez really say he's interested in me? Or did you just tell me that to see how I'd react?" We had some time. Why not dig into this stuff?

"I thought it was obvious," Nash said. "He's so into you, it practically oozes from his pores."

Ethan pointed at Nash, agreeing with him.

I frowned. "But he hasn't done anything to me."

"To you?" Nash furrowed his brow. "That's a funny way to put it."

Looking up at the ceiling as if I could see Mendez there, I tried to understand what Nash meant. Nope, I didn't. "When he helped me up and down, he didn't, you know, grab my ass or anything."

Ethan sat on the bed with a sigh. He patted the spot beside me. "Did you want him to?"

Trying to see how that mattered, I sat. "No."

"What's the problem then?" Ethan draped his arm over my shoulders and pulled me close.

He smelled like dirty socks and sweat, like he needed a shower five days ago. I probably did too. "It's not a problem, I just don't know why you think he's interested if he doesn't do things like that."

Nash blinked at me and backed away to block the door again. "I'm not equipped for this conversation right now. Maybe after a hard night's sleep."

"I got some sleep and I'm not really either, but you're

my sister, so let's at least start it." Ethan kissed the top of my head. "I'm getting the impression at least one boy has forced himself on you."

This conversation had turned in an unexpected direction, and I didn't like it. "I've never been raped." The words spilled out of my mouth so fast I barely pronounced them.

Ethan made faces that I couldn't see with my head leaning against him. I could tell because his jaw moved and he said nothing. He took a breath to speak and still said nothing. Twice.

"I don't think you're lying, Emma. But I think you're not being honest with yourself. Or maybe you're just not using the same definition for that word as I do. If you didn't want it, or if he wouldn't give up until you said yes, or if you were drunk or too tired to resist, or it happened so fast you didn't quite understand it, that's all rape. The difference between rape and not rape is consent."

My pulse sped to fifty thousand beats per second. No, I would not think about that night, or that party, or that afternoon, or that time, or those other times.

He rubbed his eyes with a finger and thumb. "I don't think we have time to get into this right now. Instead of prodding at it much, I want you to make me a promise."

I huddled on myself, terrified of what he wanted from me. This whole trip to the station had been my idea, and it had turned into a giant screw-up. They didn't want me to blame myself, I already knew that. I did anyway, because it was all my fault.

If I hadn't convinced Ethan to try this, if I hadn't gotten the wormhole to work, if, if, if, and I, I, I. Me. My fault, my responsibility.

He sighed. "Promise me you'll talk to Akata about this."

Nothing had prepared me for this promise. I thought he'd want me to bring it up another time, or think about the things that had happened to me, or something like that.

"Akata?"

"Yes. As I recall, I mentioned that she's been helping all of us avoid PTSD out here. She can help you too. Putting together everything you've learned on this mission is important. Staying sane is more important. I'd rather stay out here while Akata helps you heal than rush back home and hand you off to a therapist because I have no idea how to help you fix this."

"Seconded," Nash said from the door. "I want to go home. I miss my family, and bacon, and grits. But if staying an extra few months is all we need to get you what you need, then damn, girl, we can stay for a while."

Ethan squeezed me. "We might have to talk Baldwin into it, but I'm sure he'll come around."

We didn't have time for me to cry. They wanted me to get the help I needed from someone they trusted to get it right. And they would put off getting what they wanted for that to happen. No one had ever, ever done anything like that for me after Ethan left.

"Okay." I sniffled "I promise."

"Then we should get out of this hellhole as soon as possible. Mendez says they're ready to start." He pressed the button on the side of his neck. "On my mark." Two seconds passed. "Go."

I had the best brother in the universe. And the best Marines in the universe. Going home would ruin everything, but they wanted to go, so I'd go with them. What would I do out here by myself anyway? Roam the galaxy with Akata until I died with just her for company?

So many stupid, useless things had drifted through my head on this station. Ethan had called it a hellhole more than once, and I agreed with him.

"This is going to work."

Ethan nodded. "Yes. It will."

I believed him. Me, I couldn't believe. But him? Yes.

CHAPTER 22

We heard a voice on the PA system announce something. Nash cracked open the door and peeked through, then he slowly, gently closed it. He laid his ear against it.

I suspected the announcement had summoned everyone who could go to deal with Mendez and Baldwin. Despite all the surveillance, these aliens didn't have great person-to-person communication. Or maybe they didn't have a way to blast a message to everybody at once through their personal radios?

Once again, they had different priorities. The Marines' radios kept everyone connected whether they wanted it or not. These aliens had some other preference.

Nash waited half a minute, then he checked outside the door again. This time, he opened it. Instead of saying anything, he waved for us to follow as he stepped through.

I stayed behind Ethan with my taser ready. Using it still made me squeamish, but at least now I knew I could do it.

Later, I'd worry about what that meant.

We ran along the wall to the docking corridor. Once we reached the open doorway, Nash slipped to the other side. He peered up the corridor in one direction while Ethan checked the other. They both flashed a thumbs-up.

Mendez and Baldwin had emptied the docking corridor. Whatever they'd done, it had certainly gotten the aliens' attention.

"You'll know if they get hurt, right?"

Ethan nodded to me as we stepped into the corridor and put a finger to his lips. "They're fine," he whispered.

Right. Stealthy. Sorry.

Staying close to the wall, I jogged in their wake.

Nash collided with an alien rushing down the stairs. They bounced off each other. The alien fell down the rest of the stairs. Nash hit the wall. Ethan leaped around the corner and zapped someone.

I zapped the alien on the ground. My arm jerked upward, I aimed, and I pushed the button. Without a lot of thought, even. Seeing Ethan and Nash in danger, and knowing I had a way to help, I reacted.

My reaction hadn't involved screaming, panicking, running away, or covering my face. I'd gulped in a sharp breath of surprise, but nothing more.

For good measure, I zapped the alien again.

Nash reached over and pushed my arm down. "Twice is plenty," he murmured.

"Cog, get down to the airlock while we stow these bodies." Ethan dragged his alien down the stairs by their feet. The alien's face bonked on each step. I had a feeling he did that on purpose.

"We could just leave 'em," Nash said.

I ran at full speed and didn't hear Ethan's response. The idea of reaching the safety of Akata's internals propelled me like fire under my feet. Nothing else mattered until I got inside that ship. Passing the first docking door, I counted the seconds until I'd reach her.

Wait.

The sentinels had acquired Akata as a target before that first alien ship had docked. They could control the weapons from the ships.

Oh, crap.

If either ship had anyone on board, they could fire on

Akata and hit her. I reached up to press the button on my neck for my mic, but I didn't have it anymore. I'd have to wait for Ethan and Nash.

Slowing to a stop, I returned to that first docking door and slapped the green button. By the time the door opened, Ethan led Nash to join me.

"What are you doing?" Ethan asked, trying to hustle me along. "Akata is on the end."

"They can control the sentinels from the ships."

Nash opened his mouth, then he shut it. Ethan blinked at me.

"This one is small, and I already know the layout." I pointed at the second green light. "That's the one they used to tractor beam Akata over here."

Ethan rubbed his face. Maybe he swore under his breath. "Okay. We can go through both of them together."

Not sure I knew why I offered to do this, I gulped and said, "It'll go faster if we split up."

"She can zap an alien," Nash said. "I just watched her do it."

"I can do this. It's the size of a fishing boat." Why did I argue to go alone? What the actual heck happened in my brain? "I've already been on it. Even if there are aliens, it can only fit a few."

Ethan let out a breath and shook his head. "Okay." He didn't look like he accepted this idea. He looked like he wanted to tell me to go to my room and think about what I'd done. Jabbing a finger at me, he said, "But you go straight to Akata when you're done sweeping the ship and vandalizing the controls. Don't even look at the second ship. You don't have a radio, so we might shoot you by accident."

Weird things happened inside my belly and chest. Everything fluttered and swelled and panicked and sang at the same time. "Smash screens." Did my voice tremble? I hoped not. "They do everything with screens."

Ethan pulled me into a quick hug, then he let go and

ran up the corridor. Nash flashed me an approving grin with a thumbs up and followed Ethan.

I, the crazy person, rushed inside the airlock. As I darted through the ship door, I fished in my bag for my scissors.

Not every screen needed smashing. I would remember that. The one next to the airlock, for example, should stay intact.

At the door to the control room, I paused and wished these aliens used windows sometimes. Not everywhere, but a view through the door would've been nice.

Anyone inside would notice the door opening a crack. No point in alerting them to my presence before I could zap them.

Breathe.

I cranked the handle, flung the door open, and pointed my taser into the room.

Two aliens stood inside, both facing the back wall. They jumped, startled by my abrupt entrance. My eyes felt like they popped out of their sockets. Did my mouth open to scream? No. I shouted at them, in a wordless cry of something other than fear.

I wrenched the button on the taser. One alien spasmed and fell to the floor. The other squeaked and fumbled at his belt.

Every square inch of my body shook. I jerked my hand to the side to target the second alien. By then, he'd freed his own taser. We pointed our weapons at each other. I met his gaze.

Written across his face, he had the same kind of shocky panic I felt. This guy probably fixed machines or did some other support job. Like me. He didn't have battle training or war-honed reflexes. Neither did I. His hand shook as he held the weapon. So did mine.

We both gasped for breath like we'd each run a marathon in the past five seconds.

He considered me inferior because I was human. But we were the same. Aside from the skin tone and antennae, language, and culture, we both had blood and bones. We both wanted to live. Each of us had hopes and dreams, families and friends. Different shells, same insides.

Maybe he had two heart organs or something else instead of kidneys, or whatever.

We were the same.

Almost.

He enabled slavery. I wanted freedom.

I pushed the button. He didn't. Because I wanted it more.

"Sorry," I said as he collapsed in pain. Did I really feel sorry? Maybe? I didn't like causing anyone pain. The expressions on their faces as these two watched me, unable to do anything else, made me cringe.

To keep them down and make them stop watching me, I zapped both again. Their eyes fluttered shut. Thank goodness.

With my trusty scissors, I smashed every screen. Glass sprinkled over the two unconscious aliens without hurting them. This guy would have a story to tell, if the shame of the situation didn't stop him.

As soon as the room had no more intact screens in reach, I leaped for the door. Then I changed my mind and stole the tasers from both aliens. For good measure, I patted them down and stole everything in their pockets. Part of me wanted to abduct one of these guys and see how they felt about it. Akata and I could learn their language. We could turn him to our side.

Except I didn't want to make a decision like that for the whole group. Bringing an alien on board sounded like it would involve dangers I couldn't imagine or grasp. Especially for Akata.

Not this time. Even though I had a great candidate for it lying at my feet, I wouldn't try to drag him down to the airlock and then explain to Ethan. He'd have to think about it and get everyone's vote. Akata deserved a chance to have a say. Mendez and Baldwin might need to stay quiet.

But gosh, I had a great opportunity right here.

CHAPTER 23

I dragged him out of the ship and down the corridor to the airlock. The effort cost me a lot, and we'd probably wind up leaving him there, but I'd torture myself with missed possibilities if I didn't at least ask everyone. We could learn so much from him.

Leaving him on the floor, I slapped the button for Akata's airlock. It opened on both ends. Akata's outer hull, a bumpy red-brown surface, hovered a foot from the open door at the end.

As a side note, I still didn't quite understand how she did that. The field surrounding her acted like an airlock. Somehow. Magic, for all I knew. Something something sufficiently advanced technology and all that.

Standing at the end, I reached out and touched her hull. The surface made my hand tingle with the chill. Then I took a deep breath and shouted her name as loud as I could.

I did not look down. Gravity wouldn't suck me into space, and I knew that. If I stepped off the end, Akata's outer field would keep me buoyed in place. But I still didn't look down at the empty gap between the end of the airlock and her hull. Because I might've faltered too much.

She did nothing. No reaction. I patted her hull. Then I thumped on it. "Akata, it's Emma." Could she hear me? Could she see me? Was she mad? Was she still unconscious? "I'm so sorry I got you hurt. I was cut off from the guys, and I forgot about the guns. It was dumb. I should've found a way to shut them down before sending you a message, but all I could think about was…me, I guess."

Hanging my head, I closed my eyes so I wouldn't see the stars below. "We can't do this without you. Please let me in. Please. We're running out of options on the station. The wormhole device is broken and I don't know how to fix it. These blue-skin people know we're here, and I even found one who might be a repair tech to bring, in case you're willing to take him and help us learn the language.

"And I know it's not fair to ask for that when you'll probably have to do all the work, and no one else knows yet, but I'm asking anyway because I really want to help these guys get home. They deserve it. No matter how much I'd rather stay with you for the rest of my life, it wouldn't be right to ignore a potential advantage just because I hate everything back home."

"Cog," Ethan said, behind me. "Do you mean that?"

Right now, I did. In my heart, I never wanted to go home. Even if it meant watching Ethan disappear through the wormhole and staying by myself, I wanted to stay here. I'd go through it anyway because if they all did, I'd have to. What I wanted and what I got had never meshed before. Why should they start now?

I nodded. One last time, I patted Akata's hull. "Please let us in."

The hull parted with an agonizing lack of speed. My entire being flooded with relief. I hadn't killed her.

As soon as I could, I leaped across and touched the inner wall. "I'm so sorry, Akata. I'm so, so sorry." Leaning my forehead against the warm, live blood coral wall, I wanted to crawl inside and be enveloped.

Blood coral, its rich red glorious after so much gray, streamed up my arm and across my body to cover me in an armored coating. As soon as the coral reached the back of my neck, Akata could speak to me through my spine. For now, she left my face uncovered.

"My systems are not responding as swiftly as I wish at the moment." Her voice after all this time, streaming into my head without bothering my ears, filled me with joy. "I did not mean to leave you standing there for so long. Of course you made a mistake. I did not suspect for one moment you had neglected to disable the guns on purpose."

"I'm so glad you were only stunned." I couldn't keep myself from crying anymore. Tears streamed down my cheeks.

"As am I. What is the situation?"

I told her. While I didn't need to speak out loud to communicate with her, it helped me calm down and didn't feel so weird as thinking at her.

"I can restrain this alien for you. His language would be a valuable addition to my catalog. And I believe that with the right incentives, you could convince him to turn traitor against his people. Have Harper and Nash bring him. Then we will go pick up Mendez and Baldwin and escape the area before any station repairs can be made."

Looking up, I saw Ethan watching me with a frown from the other side of the airlock. Nash crouched over the downed alien, his attention on the corridor.

"Bring the alien." I beckoned them forward. "She's a little slow, but fine."

Ethan hefted the alien over his shoulder while Nash watched his back. They jogged up the airlock. I stood aside. They hopped across the gap.

"We're inside, Akata. Let's go get the others." He patted her wall.

"I have no way to express how happy I am to see you, Akata," Nash said.

The hull shut.

"Have him set the prisoner on the floor," Akata said. "I will take him."

I relayed the request. Ethan dumped the alien on the floor without regard for their safety.

"We abducted an alien what abducted aliens," Nash said. "Seems like closing a circle or somesuch."

The blood coral crept around the alien's body and dragged him under the surface.

"He is secure," Akata said.

I nodded and wiped my face with a coral-covered hand. The surface absorbed my tears. "Can you get free of the cables around the ship?"

"One way to find out."

"Akata," Ethan said, "We need the spare weapons." He glanced at me, and I couldn't tell what he felt. Some kind of confusion over how to deal with me, for sure, but I couldn't read the rest. "We'll talk later, Cog."

Two rifles, copies of those the guys had lost, emerged from the wall. Ethan passed one to Nash and took one for himself. I already knew I couldn't lift the sleek, alien things, so I held up one of my three tasers.

"Cog, if you want, you can relax now. Get some sleep. I said you could, so you can."

The ship shifted as Akata moved to untangle herself from the cables holding her in place. Whatever happened, the blood coral armor could keep me stable and rooted in place.

As much as I knew I needed the sleep, I felt kind of wired and ready to storm the station. That would probably wear off soon. "Are Mendez and Baldwin in trouble?"

"Might as well ask if pigs like mud," Nash muttered.

A picture of Mendez and Baldwin playing in mud like a swimming pool flashed into my head. Mendez had no shirt on, which took the idea in an unexpected direction. Especially since I hadn't seen any of these guys shirtless. The version of him in my head reminded me of an underwear model. With great abs.

Way to get distracted, Emma. "Then I'll help. I have armor now, and Akata in my ear."

"She's got a taser and she knows how to use it," Nash said. He nudged Ethan in the side.

Ethan rolled his eyes. "You're both too tired for this, but stay up if you want."

"The cables have not hampered me," Akata said. "They merely required some maneuvering to free myself. I do not believe they had any idea what I am capable of."

"Probably not." I flashed a thumbs up at Ethan. "Akata says she's free. We're proceeding to the other airlock."

Ethan pushed the button on his neck. "Akata is loose and we're on our way. Status report." He looked at the floor while listening. His face drew into a deep frown.

"That's no good," Nash muttered.

"What's no good? What's going on?" If I wanted to, I could ask Akata to get me a spare radio from storage so I could listen in. This wouldn't take long, though, right? Akata would sidle up to the airlock, the hull would open, and we'd provide cover fire. Mendez and Baldwin would jump in. We'd flee for the safety of elsewhere.

Waving for me to stop talking, Ethan asked, "Is there a back way out?" He listened. "Best guess on how many?"

I needed a radio. Without opening my mouth, I asked Akata to get one for me by picturing it. The guys never saw, even if they looked, because she brought it to me through the armor. If they'd watched, they would've seen the bulge climb up my body from the floor, but they had more important things to focus on.

"—leave without us," Mendez said. He whispered and sounded desperate.

"Out of the question," Ethan said, both beside me and into my ear. "Nash, are you up for a smash and grab?"

"For them? I'm up to storming the citadel."

"I'm coming too," I said, using the mic so they all knew I had it. Unlike them, I only had to signal Akata mentally if I wanted to turn it on or off. This beat standard hands-free operation.

All four of them, in unison, said, "No."

Nash put a hand on my shoulder. Akata let me feel it

through the armor. "We need you to keep the last stretch clear, okay?"

"Chica, I know you want to prove yourself," Mendez whispered. "That's great. This isn't the time or place. This isn't just a single alien with his back to the door. We're outnumbered by a lot, and they've got a bunch of robots. Maybe you'd do fine, but we can't take the chance that you'll freeze up, or be too tired not to hit one of us with your taser. If it was about figuring out how to make a device work, that'd be you. This, though, is our thing. Stay back and keep the exit clear. Okay?"

I looked at Ethan, hoping he'd see how much I could help.

He didn't. "He's right, Cog. You're not trained for this. Besides, providing cover while we evacuate is an important job. I know you can do that, which means both Nash and I can go rescue Mendez and Baldwin."

"Rescue is a little strong there, boss," Mendez said.

Nash snorted. "If you hadn't got your dumb ass into a sling, you wouldn't need that strong a word."

"Okay," I said with a meek nod. They had a point, and I could do the job they needed. "I'll be here."

And then I watched them leap across the gap, rifles ready, to go save Mendez and Baldwin. While I listened, unable to help.

CHAPTER 24

The guys might as well have used a different language once they forgot about me listening. I understood the numbers, and got the basic idea, at least. The specifics flew over my head. Mostly, I wanted to know if any of them took a hit or needed me to come help. So I paid attention and tried to sort out the situation.

Mendez and Baldwin had succeeded beyond their wildest dreams, pulling at least two dozen aliens into pursuit of them. They'd also attracted six or seven robots, all attempting to follow their programming to apprehend specimens of races other than the blue-skin people.

"Akata," I said without activating the mic. "I know how to turn off those robots, but I'd have to go into the station again."

"I remember the room with the screens. You were ordered to stay here, though." She could stop me if she wanted to. Part of her coral colony covered my entire body.

"With your help, I could get there and back before they do."

"I believe it would be wiser for you to remain here."

Probably true. Strange that I kept wanting to rush into danger and perform daring deeds. Worse, I wanted to go back after finally escaping. What caused that? Lack of food diversity? Not enough rest? I wondered if, after getting enough sleep, all the things I'd done on the station would horrify me.

"Can you check if the prisoner knows another way to disable the robots?"

"Not while standing ready to leave on short notice. Accessing him will require time and attention on my part, just as it does for all of you."

Next time. Everything I'd learned would apply next time, not this time. So frustrating. I wanted to help, but had no options.

"Emma," Mendez murmured. "I can hear you fretting through the mic."

Someone chuckled.

"You've already done a lot today." Mendez paused. I heard nothing for several seconds. "We almost got home because of you, and now we know you can make it work another time. You got us out of that prison cell. You sent a message to Akata. You crawled around in the guts of this place to get all this stuff done and made everything possible."

"A-damned-men," Nash said.

They quieted for several seconds again.

A flurry of whispers chased each other, and I couldn't tell who said what. They fell into that code stuff again, so I had no real idea what happened. Then the whispers stopped and I heard nothing for a long time.

I doubted the aliens had done anything on purpose to make the radios stop transmitting. More likely, the guys needed both hands to handle their situations. Which meant I got to wait, imagining the worst.

Pacing across the entry, I chewed my lip and tried not to fidget too much.

"What I'm saying is," Mendez said. Then nothing. His voice had sounded strained. With pain? Weariness? Frustration?

"Mendez is hit," Baldwin said.

This news hit me like a punch to the gut. I gasped for

breath and needed to do something. Mendez never got hit. Everyone else did, but not him. He wouldn't die. The aliens didn't kill people, they threw people into boxes and turned them into slaves.

"Akata, we have to help them."

"I do not have any new suggestions."

Hugging myself, I tried to think of something, anything I could do. I didn't know where to find the guys. Akata had no weapons of her own. The taser in my hand scrambled the electrical impulses in organic bodies enough to stun them.

Tasers functioned by producing an electrical charge. In most systems, an unexpected electrical charge caused a surge. Systems could shield from surges. Compared to the engines on this station, the tasers barely tickled, but the wiring was another story.

I had three tasers.

"I have an idea," I told Akata. "It might do something, and it might do nothing. But it won't take me far from the door. I just need a crowbar."

"Very well. I will not stop you from making your attempt." After a few moments, the wall produced a crowbar.

"Thanks." With the crowbar in hand, I leaped across the gap to re-enter the station. Only a few feet from the open door, I dropped to one knee. For unknown reasons, the flooring in this section had electrified grates. The rest of the station didn't, but this part did.

Using the crowbar, and shielded from shocks by the coral armor, I heaved against a section of the floor. The coral helped. We pried up a floor section.

These idiots really needed to learn about rivets. They hadn't even used sealant on these floor panels. Morons.

They could punch holes in time and space. That didn't make them smart.

I picked up the crowbar. To my surprise, the coral took it from me, and the crowbar became a bulge along the outside of my thigh.

Cool.

At my mental request, Akata helped me retrieve my three tasers. I held all three in two hands.

"I see your intent," Akata said. "The suit can deliver synchronized blasts."

"Go ahead." I had to stand close, so I bent my knees and stood tense, ready to sprint away from an explosion or other disaster.

The coral held the tasers between my hands. More coral crept over my face, protecting every inch of me except my eyes. Though this restricted my hearing, I thought that might help while we tried to cause a power surge. Besides, I could still hear the guys in the earbud just fine.

Akata activated all three tasers at once and sent three jolts of electricity into the grid under the floor. Sparks leaped from the impact point. Around me, the light flickered and dimmed.

The tasers fired again. This time, sparks popped and flew higher. Lights failed, replaced by the dim red glow of automation and emergencies.

"The circuit is blown," Akata said. "Another jolt may have no effect."

"Try it anyway."

Once more, the three tasers blasted the exposed wiring. In the distance, something snapped and popped.

"What just happened?" Ethan asked.

"Do it again," I told Akata.

She jolted the wires again.

"Lights are out," Baldwin reported.

"Here too," Nash said.

"Nash, let's move."

"With you, boss."

My heart swelled. Staying back had forced me to think about things the way I knew how despite how much I needed sleep. "One more time, Akata, then I need to cover this and get back onto the ship."

Nash was right to question whether I'd falter or not. Maybe weariness had shown on my face. Or maybe, like the other guys, he'd known I had a different job than that. Either way, I needed to remember that I had different skills than the guys. Rushing in like a commando didn't fall under my purview. Hanging in the rear and doing stuff like this did.

With Akata's help, I replaced the floor panel. The guys stopped talking, which probably meant they'd once again shifted to using both hands for action. I returned to Akata and stowed the crowbar, plus one taser. To cover my returning Marines, I'd keep one per hand, and fire as needed.

On second thought, I crossed into the station again and stayed a step from the door. Akata would make sure I got back inside as necessary.

"Coming in hot, Cog."

I raised my tasers. "Does 'hot' mean someone lost their shirt?"

"Chica, you're hilarious." Mendez's voice held that same strained, worn quality as Ethan's had after taking a taser hit.

"Pursuit," Ethan snapped.

Nash rounded the corner, charging toward me with a determined scowl. Ethan followed close on his heels with Mendez slung over his shoulder. Baldwin came last, firing his rifle over his shoulder as he ran.

Mendez lifted his head enough to see me. He grinned like an idiot.

Nash stopped beside me and raised his rifle.

Two aliens rounded the corner. Nash fired. Ethan passed us. When I felt confident I wouldn't hit Baldwin, I pressed the buttons on both tasers.

Baldwin passed between us. A robot trundled around the corner.

When Nash stepped backward, so did I. He kept firing. I zapped again, this time switching between the two tasers.

The jolts from my tasers made the robot stutter in its progress.

Two more aliens crept forward behind the robot, using it for cover. Two could play that game. I moved so I provided Nash cover. Their taser blasts bounced off Akata's armor. They didn't bounce off Nash.

Nash put his hand on my shoulder. He held his rifle by my side and fired it. When he tugged, I understood what he wanted.

We stepped backward together.

"Cog," Ethan said into my ear. "On my mark, I want you to turn and jump into the ship.

"Understood."

Nash patted my shoulder and let go.

I kept firing. Bolts kept bouncing off the coral armor.

"Go," Ethan said.

As I turned, I saw Baldwin and Ethan standing at the hole in the hull, waiting for me to jump. I took two running steps and leaped across the gap. They caught me and pulled me in.

Akata probably did most of the work, but they'd treated me like a member of the team.

CHAPTER 25

I stumbled to a stop with Ethan and Baldwin each holding one of my arms. The hull shut. Everything except what I saw twisted in five directions at once. My stomach fluttered and flopped. I wanted to throw up and didn't dare. Tiny flickers of static edged my vision.

"You have an especially sensitive reaction to the sensation of rapid acceleration and deceleration," Akata said, noting it as if she'd mentioned the weather.

All the ickiness faded. Akata withdrew enough of her coral to leave me uncovered except for a strip along my spine and around my neck. We could still talk like this.

Mendez lay on the floor where Ethan had dropped him help catch me. Nash, on one knee beside him, gripped his hand and helped him stand. The two men grinned about something.

"We're safe now," Ethan said. He set his hands on my shoulders from behind and took a step deeper into the ship. "Everybody's earned about a year of R and R. Let's get some sleep."

I didn't know what to do or think, or how to feel or act. Seeing Mendez wobble to his feet with Nash's help and the wall's support, I had a powerful urge to run away. At the same time, I wanted to duck under his arm and help him.

Nash had him covered. None of these guys needed me.

Without my help, they eventually would've freed themselves again. Most of the disasters on the station had been my fault anyway.

Ethan walked me around the corner. I needed some sleep. Everything would suck less in the morning.

"Emma," Mendez said.

I stopped because Ethan stopped. He let out a tiny sigh. "You need rest even more than she does," he muttered.

Mendez grinned. "The thing I was trying to say before I got hit."

Not sure where this would go, I nodded.

"You're doing the engineer's job. All that stuff you did on the station, that's what the engineer does in hostile territory. We're the infantry. We shoot things and stab things, rush defenses, build barricades, keep watch. The engineer figures out stuff, screws with electronics, finds places to wiggle through where us big guys can't fit. That's you."

His words made my heart swell.

Ethan kissed the top of my head and nudged me to keep going. "He's right. Until we pulled you out here by accident, I don't think we really had a solid chance of ever getting home. Now, we do."

"We didn't have a full team," Nash said.

Baldwin grunted.

We shuffled into the sleeping chamber, a room big enough to hold five person-sized pods. One, intended for me, had a shorter bed and stood at a lower height. The rest could each take a meaty, six-foot tall war machine in combat boots.

Nash helped Mendez to the pod next to mine. Ethan let go and headed for the last pod on the end. Baldwin followed suit.

I sat on the edge of my pod, facing Mendez. My entire body drooped as I processed the reality of being safe. The danger had passed. We could all rest, knowing Akata kept vigilance over us.

Nash let go of Mendez and hopped onto his own pod.

"Night," Ethan said.

One by one, Akata closed the coral over the guys' pods until Mendez and I sat together, our knees an inch apart.

Asking him about anything felt weird and awkward. I tried to think of how to phrase a question and failed. As I hovered on the brink of giving up, Mendez set a hand on my knee.

"If now is when you need to talk, I'll listen. We might both keel over in the middle, but I'll stay awake as long as I can."

"No, it can wait." I frowned at the floor because I still didn't know what to say.

"Emma." Mendez rubbed his face with both hands, then he shook his head. "I haven't used my first name since I enlisted. It's Santiago."

I'd only met him maybe a week ago, but it already seemed weird to call him something other than Mendez. "Okay. It's nice to meet you, Santiago." Since I couldn't figure out what else to do, I offered him my hand.

We shook.

"There's something I want to say to you, but I'm not sure how to word it." Mendez kept my hand and covered it with his other one. "We've all been out here for a long time. All men. Started with twelve, down to four. You know that. Before we got thrown out here, our unit was on deployment for six months. That was our second time out, so we've all been kind of…outside regular civilization for a while."

He paused and twitched his mouth, his gaze stuck on our hands. I restrained a strange urge to touch his face.

"What I'm saying is none of us has even seen a girl in years, let alone talk to one. Or anything else. Even before we were ganked out here, we'd been in the field for a while."

I blinked at him. "Oh." This weird conversation had taken a weirder turn.

For a long moment, he stared over my shoulder as if the wall had answers or cue cards. Then he shrugged. "I can't think of any other way to say this. Maybe I'm too tired and it should wait, but this is important. I'm attracted to you, but I don't know if it's because you're the first girl I've seen in a long time, or because I'm attracted to you."

My cheeks burned with the heat of a thousand suns. I still had nothing to say because my brain wouldn't work.

"I think it makes a difference. It matters because you matter." He squeezed my hand. "Right now, the only way I can figure to tell is if I get to know you better. Which takes time, right?"

Nodding, I kept blinking like a moron. Did he see my blush? What did he think it meant? What did it mean?

"And I know you've been through a lot. Maybe your friends back home couldn't tell you're hurting on the inside, but we can. All of us could see it, even before you said anything. It's in your eyes." He let go of my hand and brushed his rough fingertips against my temple.

My heart sped to five billion beats per second as he met my gaze.

"I don't know how to fix that kind of thing. If you'll let me try, though, I'll help. Because I can see how amazing you are underneath all the pain. There's an incredible woman here, one who can do what it takes to get things done. Sometimes she forgets all the details like anyone would, but she's got plenty of courage and is about fifty times smarter than me. Maybe more."

Wound up, exhausted, confused, and struggling under whatever else pressed on my shoulders, I burst into tears.

Mendez held me while I cried. He didn't try to shush me or tell me everything is fine, or say anything else stupid. We just sat together, with his strength providing a safe haven.

When I subsided to sniffles, he kissed the side of my head. Like Ethan, he smelled like he needed a shower and clean clothes. I did too. Every part of me felt grubby.

"I'm glad you're here to save us," he murmured. "And that we can also save you."

I wanted him to kiss me. Except I also didn't. "I'm glad for that too."

He hugged me close. "Right now, we both need rest, so I'm going to help you lie down. We can talk more in the morning, okay?"

"Okay."

With his support, I leaned back in my pod. He stood over me until the pod closed, cutting off my view of anything except blood coral.

Finally, I slept. It had been a long damned day.

OTHER BOOKS BY THE AUTHOR

Harper Revolution
young adult space opera portal fantasy
Defiance (prequel coming summer 2019)
Porcelain
Crawlspace

Spirit Knights
young adult urban fantasy
Girls Can't Be Knights
Backyard Dragons
Ethereal Entanglements
Ghost Is the New Normal
Boys Can't Be Witches
War of the Rose Covens
Death and Dragons In Omaha (coming early 2020)

Fantasy in the Ilauris setting
sword and sorcery fantasy
Damsel In Distress
Shadow & Spice (short story)
Al-Kabar

Maze Beset trilogy
superhero science fiction
Dragons In Pieces
Dragons In Chains
Dragons In Flight
Superheroes in Denim (compilation)

The Greatest Sin
(with Erik Kort)
epic fantasy
The Fallen
Harbinger
Moon Shades
Illusive Echoes
A Curse of Memories

Darkside Seattle
cyberpunk for grownups
Street Doc
Fixer
Mechanic
Hacker
Meat (coming late 2019)

Anthologies
Into the Woods: a fantasy anthology
Merely This and Nothing More: Poe Goes Punk
Unnatural Dragons: a science fiction anthology
What We've Unlearned: English Class Goes Punk
Hideous Progeny: Horror Goes Punk
Enter the Aftermath
Well…It's Your Cow
Swords, Sorcery, & Self-Rescuing Damsels
Taught By Time: Mythology Goes Punk (coming late 2019)

WWW.AUTHORLEEFRENCH.COM

ABOUT THE AUTHOR

Lee French lives in Olympia, WA, with two kids, two bicycles, and too much stuff. She is an avid gamer and a member of the Myth-Weavers online RPG community. In addition to spending too much time there, she also trains in taekwondo, keeps a nice flower garden with one dragon and absolutely no lawn gnomes, works an excessive number of book events, and tries in vain every year to grow vegetables that don't get devoured by neighborhood wildlife.

She is an active member of the Science Fiction and Fantasy Writers of America and the Northwest Independent Writers Association, as well as serving the Olympia region as a NaNoWriMo Municipal Liaison.

If you enjoyed this book, please take a moment to review it wherever you purchase your books or ebooks.